# ISLE OF
# INNOCENCE

TREASURED LOVE COLLECTION

# ISLE OF
# INNOCENCE

LEEANNA NEECE

# OTHER BOOKS IN THE
# TREASURED LOVE COLLECTION

Palmetto Publishing Group, LLC
Charleston, SC

For information regarding special discounts or for bulk purchases, please contact Palmetto Publishing Group at Info@PalmettoPublishingGroup.com.


ISBN-13: 978-1-944313-03-6
ISBN-10: 1944313036

*I dedicate this book to my husband, who has stood by me through all the late nights, writer's blocks, and has helped me run through ideas. He is my best friend and my everything. Thank you for being there for me.*

# TABLE OF CONTENTS

# *Chapter* 1

The island was coming to life for the party. Spirits would normally be running high, but not this time. The women were upset because the men would be leaving the next day. Even Bre felt down. She had enjoyed having her husband home with her and their son. She couldn't place the strange feeling she got from everyone, so she worked on anything to keep her mind off that odd vibe.

That night at the party, everyone was happy. They would be leaving the next day and were ready to get back out to sea. All the women spent their last night with their men, dancing and laughing, trying to gather memories in those last moments.

Bre was talking to Wendy, making sure they had plenty of rum for the ship. She was trying to keep her spirits up, but she knew that watching Evans leave the next day would be one of the hardest things she'd do. She didn't want her worry and pain to show. Just then, Evans came over and whispered in her ear that it was time. She felt the lump in her throat fall to her stomach. This was the speech that would end the night, and she wanted the night to last as long as possible.

With Bre at his side, holding their son, Evans gathered everyone around and got their attention. "Thank you all for being here tonight. I'd like to start out by saying this: It has been a great honor sailing with all of you. I could have never asked for a better crew to call family. However, it is time for me to retire."

Everyone, including Bre, just stared at him as if he'd gone mad; then everyone began talking at the same time. Evans looked over to Bre and saw the surprise in her beautiful blue eyes, which had gone from shining and sparkling to something altogether new.

"All right, let me finish," he said, still looking at his wife; then he turned back to the crowd. "Hoss, will you and Steven come here?" Once they were at his side, Evans smiled at them. "Hoss will be the captain of *The Sphinx*. I hope that you will treat him as your captain, and have his back as you had mine. I trust him with my life, and now with all of yours."

He turned to Steven, then back to the crowd. "Steven will be the captain of *The Phoenix*; he, too, will make a fine captain, but it will be your duty to make sure he doesn't get you all into trouble. I'll let you all make your decisions, and then you can tell the captain of your choice that you will be sailing for him.

"Let's eat! Then we'll turn this into a party like none we've had before," Evans said as he looked over at his wife, who was fighting back tears.

"Why didn't you tell me?" she ask as they walked toward a table.

"I wanted it to be a surprise," he said with a smile.

"I love you, Evans, but I don't want you to give up the sea for me. It's not too late to change this."

"No," he said, hiding the hurt he felt because of his decision. "I'll be fine." He paused, then said, "If you don't mind, I need to talk to my cousin's Jerry and Ray."

Bre went straight to her father-in-law, who stood talking to his nephew, Jim. "You have to stop him," she declared. "He's making a huge mistake."

"You of all people know when Evans makes up his mind, whether it be good or bad, there's no changing it," Jim said.

"There has to be something we can do. He'll never be the same," Bre cried out, fighting back tears, but one of them slipped and began running down her cheek.

"Are you doing this because you love him and only want what's best for him, or because you feel like he'll resent you for this?" Darrell asked as he wiped away the tear from his daughter-in-law's cheek.

"Because I love him and want what's best for him."

He took his grandson from her arms. "Then I'll fix it first thing in the morning. Jim, I'll need your help, and neither of you say a word. I got him; go do something to get your mind off all this."

"Thank you," Bre said, hugging them both before walking off to find her husband.

"Would you like to dance with your wife?" she asked him from behind.

They began to dance, and as he looked at her, he could see she was deep in thought. "Princess, it's not going to be as bad as you think."

"Shh!" she said to him. "We aren't going to talk about it anymore. I just wish you had told me before tonight, but it's okay. Now dance with me, before I find someone else who will!" She flashed a grin at him.

He held her tight to him, and whispered, "That would be over my dead body," as he spun her in his arms. She let out a laugh that he loved, and his mind went free of everything. He was lost in the moment with her.

After a couple of dances, Hoss walked over to them. "It's time," he said, walking on toward the other men. Evans kissed Bre and told her he would be back in a few minutes. Then he joined the rest of the men.

Darrell led them into his office and smiled. "All right, I want to say that this will be a good year for us. I don't want any of you to stray and go back to your old ways—is that understood?"

"You mean act like Raymond and you used to?" Hoss said with a laugh.

Darrell gave Hoss a wicked smile. "Back to the business at hand, not a bunch of silly rumors you children made up about my crew. Hoss, you are now the captain of *The Sphinx*. I need your crew to sign here," he said as he laid down the oath for the ship.

Darron, Frank, Dean, Old Man Billy, and Ronnie moved to the desk and took turns placing their mark on the scroll. Then they took their places at Hoss's side.

"All right, who is who?" Darrell asked Hoss, looking at the latter's trusted crew mate's.

"Darron is my first mate, and Ronnie is my second mate. The rest will be figured out later."

"Here are your papers. You'll pick up your load here, and go from there. I'll see you back in a few months. Safe passage, my son," he said, shaking Hoss's hand. "I'll take care of him," he whispered, as he knew Hoss was worried about his brother.

"Thanks," he said as he took the papers from Ray.

Darrell turned to Steven, saying, "So I guess the rest of these cutthroats are going with you. Here are your papers; men, make your mark here."

Once the men were finished, Darrell smiled at them. "Now go enjoy the rest of your night.

"Evans, I need to speak to you for a moment." After the room had been cleared, Darrell turned to his son. "I wish you had changed your mind. I don't like this. Some of them aren't ready to be alone."

"They'll be fine," Evans said, although he knew his father was right. "Like I told you, it's not fair to my family to leave them here to worry if I'll return. It's also not fair to the men, for me to be worried about if Bre's okay, and not being able to give the crew the captain it needs."

"I understand, son, but it's not too late. We can fix this."

"No," Evans said, taking a deep breath. "I knew this was going to be hard, but it's the right thing, Dad.

"I need some air. Let Bre know I'll be back soon."

Evans left through the back and went to the only place he knew he could be free. She would understand what he was going through when no one else could. He climbed onto *The Nitingale* and walked around the top deck. She was a piece of art, and he would miss the nights they had spent on the open sea.

He was opening his mouth to talk to her when he heard the men coming aboard.

"We knew we'd find you here," Hoss said as he handed over a bottle of rum. "Figure this is the best place to celebrate our last night together, before we split once and for all."

Just then Jerry and Ray joined them. "Reckoned this is where you cutthroats went," Ray said with a laugh.

"Remember that time when nothing would do Evans, and he had to have this ship?" Jerry busted out into laughter.

Hoss spoke up. "Think that was the last time we were in this same mood. That was hard, when they split us up."

"Aye, but this time is different," Ronnie added. "This time it was one of *us* that did the splitting, not the big boss."

"We survived it then, we'll survive it this time," Evans said.

"Aye, but we sure did have some good times," Steven said as he looked around.

"That we did," Darron joined in. "Remember the time we went to that one island, and Evans got us into a fight over not having any rum?"

The men busted out in laughter and began swapping their favorite stories.

Evans walked over to the helm, with Hoss right behind him. "What's to happen to her now?" Hoss asked.

"Nothing. She'll sit right here in dry dock until the time comes for me to go back out."

"Evans, you know that once you place this in dry dock, she'll never come back."

"Hoss, stop," Evans said to him, then placed his hands on the wheel one last time.

Just then Evans, master carpenter, Cliff walked up and smiled at them. "Hey, she's able to sail. Let's take her out for a last spin."

"Aye," Hoss said, smiling as he began dishing out orders. The men all smiled and went to work.

Bre watched from a distance as *The Nitingale* left the dock. She knew that Evans needed time alone with his men, and his ship, one last time. She was pleased that he had time with them, but she felt guilty all the same. Because if it wasn't for her, he would never give his life on the sea up, and that if it weren't for her, he'd be leaving in the morning light. With his crew and his beloved ship.

"She is something else," Jim said, walking up from behind her and causing her to jump; she'd been in her own little world. "Evans picked out the finest two ladies to love."

She smiled and then turned to him. "What have I done?" she asked as tears began to run down her face.

"Stop it," Jim said. "You didn't do anything. Evans made this decision, not you."

"But he did it because of me," she said, trying to stop the tears.

"Jim glanced around sheepishly, rocking on his heels, without a clue of what to do". He looked around to find someone who could help, but he didn't see anyone. So he gently placed his arm around Bre's shoulders and pulled her to him. "Princess, please stop crying."

"I'm sorry," she said as she wiped her face. "Have the two of you come up with a plan?"

"Aye, we have the perfect plan to show him that he made the wrong decision."

They heard from behind them and both turned around; Her father-in-law walked up, reaching out with his handkerchief and wiping away her tears. Then with a stern look, he asked Jim what he'd done to make her cry.

"It wasn't Jim," she said in a hurry. "He was trying to make me stop. It's all because I ruined Evans's life," she said as she began sobing again. Now both the men felt helpless.

Darrell yelled out to his wife, who came over, looked at Bre, and smacked both of the men. "Two great captains of the sea—would fight hurricanes, armies, and anything else, but can't handle a woman's tears. I got this; now go and figure out how to fix this," she said as she took Bre and disappeared through the crowd.

"If Evans ever finds out what we're doing, he'll kill us," Jim said, glancing at Darrell.

"Aye, but it's for his own good. Plus, this will help me convince him to stay on the seas. We need the ship, along with Evans on the sea. I can give him short hauls so he can be home more."

"I don't think that's the problem, Unc. I think the problem is he's scared of what might happen." Jim shivered for even thinking about it.

"That's why it's always important to put the past behind us and turn to the upside of sailing. That way no one hangs for being pirates, and no one has to look over their shoulder for trouble."

"We'll always look over our shoulders. We've pissed off a lot of people in our lives. As long as *The Nitingale* is on the water, someone will try to destroy her. *That's* what Evans is worried about: being killed and leaving his princess and their son alone, all because his past caught up to him."

"Aye," he said in almost a whisper.

"Did you figure out if that problem I brought to you was true or not?"

"Aye, it's true. He is Evans's son. He'll be here on the next ship arriving from Virginia."

"I hate to be around this place once Bre finds out her mighty captain has a son with a barmaid." Jim busted out into laughter.

"Me too. I figure, when he gets back I can introduce them to each other."

"When it rains it pours," Jim said, watching Bre dance with her father.

The party ended, everyone went home, and only a few lingered. Bre helped clean things up until her mother-in-law ordered her off to bed. She didn't protest—just went upstairs.

She checked on her son, then went to her room and changed into her nightshirt. She walked through the long white curtains, that was gently blowing in the breeze. Once she was on the balcony, she could smell the islands exotic flowers mixed with the smell of salt in the air. She looked out into the horizon to watch *The Nitingale* float in the distance. She wrapped her arms around her round shoulders and held tight to herself, as she watched the ship, and let the tears flow.

Bre woke up the next morning. She looked around and saw her husband's glass lying on the nightstand. She smiled. Some things will never change, she thought to herself. After quickly dressing, she walked into her son's room and saw he was already gone.

She loved that she had help, and would miss it when everyone left, but she was ready to be alone with her husband and son. She hurried downstairs and found all the family, but Evans at the table.

"He said he was going to the docks," her brother Brandon said without looking up.

"Thank you," she said as she retrieved her son from her mother-in-laws lap, and headed toward the door.

"Where are you going?" her father asked.

"I need to be there to tell the men goodbye. It's a custom, and I don't want to change anything."

"Wait!" her brother Pike called out. He jumped up with his two brothers, and they all headed to the docks.

"Morning, my princess," Evans said with a half smile as Bre walked up to him, holding their son in her arms.

"Morning, my captain." She smiled, trying to test his mood. "I noticed you came home last night. I thought you might stay out there forever."

"Aye, and I noticed that my wife had been crying. We'll talk about that later," he said with a flash in his eyes.

"Aye," she replied weakly. That was one argument, about her crying she wanted to avoid.

He noticed her expression change and pulled her to him. "It will be all right, princess. I'm where I want and need to be."

She could feel the tears coming again, and she fought them as hard as she could, but was failing. When he pulled her by her shoulders to look at her face, she saw the fire in his eyes. "I love you," was all she said to him.

He again held her close to him, without saying a word, as if he knew her agony. She blamed herself for his decision, and he had to find a way to let her know it would be all right. Yes, he could have stayed on the sea, but he didn't want to. He wanted to be with her and his family. How could he make her understand that it had nothing to do with her coming into his life?

"Stop blaming yourself, princess. I made up my mind on this, and it had nothing to do with you."

"Aye, it did," she said, looking up at him.

"Well, some of it, but it's me. I can't be out there and leave you here. So let it go, princess, and be happy that I'm not like them," he said, watching the men load boxes and trunks onto the ship.

"Aye." She forced a smile, reached up, and gave him a kiss. "Go— you are needed over there. We'll be here waiting to say our goodbyes."

"First," he said, smiling. He reached down and kissed her softly, then delved deeper, into a passionate kiss. Pulling away, he looked into her blue eyes. He brushed away a strand of her hair, placing it gently behind her ear. "Princess, I love you, and I'm happy being with you. I will do whatever it takes to show you that you're not responsible for this. So please stop blaming yourself. If I see tears again in those beautiful eyes, I'll bend you over my knee and give you a true reason to have them."

"Aye," she said, smiling at him. "I love you, my mighty captain." She reached up and kissed him once again. "Now go and be with your men. I'll join you in a moment."

The men were preparing to set sail. Evans tried to help them and act happy about it, but he hated that he wasn't going. He loved his life and didn't want to change anything about it, but the sea had a hold on him that even Bre couldn't compare to.

Hoss had *The Sphinx* loaded and was ready and happy to leave. But even his happiness couldn't conceal that he hated the fact that the crew was splitting up. This was the first time since they began sailing the seas, that they'd be going their separate ways. He'd never thought it would happen; he always assumed they'd be together until they were too old to sail. He wasn't sure if he'd be able to walk away from plundering. It was in his blood, and in the men's blood, but he'd given his word. Even when all else failed, he'd keep his word.

He smiled when Steven walked over to them. Even if Steven was an aggravating little shit, Hoss would miss him.

Evans gathered the men together and told them to be careful. As he said his goodbyes, he had a feeling in his stomach that something wasn't right.

"I know that look," Hoss said from behind him. "I have it, too. I think it's from us going our separate ways, and leaving you behind."

"I was hoping you'd come to your senses and be leaving with us," Ronnie said as he slapped Evans on his back.

"Can't—this is where I belong now," he replied and looked over at Bre, who stood on the dock holding their little boy.

"It will be a shame to not have you with us," Ronnie said as he looked over at Bre, "but I can't say I blame you." Then he left, joining his family to say bye to them.

Mike and Dean walked over to Evans. "We'll miss you. Take care of Sandy," Mike said as he went to board the ship.

"Tell him I will, Dean, and I'll look after Heather for you as well."

"I know you will." Then Dean joined Mike to finish preparations.

Glover walked over. As he told them goodbye, he looked over at Evans. "Man, I'll miss you," he said before boarding the ship.

That left only Darron and Hoss.

Darron looked toward Steven's ship. "Who'll take care of him now?"

"Hopefully Steven has learned enough to stay out of trouble," Hoss said.

"He hasn't," Bre said as she joined them.

"You aren't making this easy for us," Hoss said as he looked at her.

"He'll be fine. He has Danny and Glover to keep him in line," Evans lied.

Hoss just stared at him. "I hope you're right, man. I hate to see you wrong."

"Me too," Evans said, almost whispering.

"All right, the ship is ready to pick up our load and the crew," Darron announced. He turned to Evans. "It's going to be hard to start calling him 'Captain.' When there's only one Cap. Take care, man."

"Hoss, take care," Bre said as she reached up to hug him.

"I will, princess." Then he turned to his friend. "This is the first time in years that we won't be together. I'll miss you," he said, hating himself for saying it.

"I'll miss you as well. Now go and be the cap we both know you are," Evans said as he slapped his brother on his back.

Hoss looked one last time to Steven, then back at Evans. "This shit isn't right." He left before anything else could be said.

"I know," Evans said to himself. He watched as they left, then turned to Bre and saw her looking at him.

"It will be fine. Hoss is ready for this," she said. She knew the entire situation was killing him.

"Well, we're off," Steven said as he walked up to Evans. "Sorry I had to disappear, but I had to make sure everything was set. I hate that I didn't get to tell Hoss bye. Maybe I'll run into him."

"Steven, please stay out of trouble," Evans said. "We aren't the same anymore. You won't have *The Nitingale* to protect you."

"Stop worrying. I'll be fine." Then he gave Evans a hug then jumped onto his ship as it began moving away from the docks." he said with a laugh.

Only Bre and Evans remained. She stood tall by her husband's side; she knew he was hurting. A part of him wished he were with the others on *The Nitingale*, while the other part was where he wanted to be.

The ships were out of their sight, but he still stood there, looking out to the water.

"We have this, Bre," Ray said as he, Jerry, and Rod walked up. "We'll take care of him. He might be in late and a lot drunk." Jerry smiled at her.

"Thanks," she said, looking over at Evans and then back at the men. "Well he be fine?"

"I *am* fine. Don't worry, princess. I knew this was going to be hard, but it's worth it, to be with you and our son. Go and take care of him, and stop worrying about me."

She reached over to kiss him and then she left. She hadn't known until that moment how hard it had been for him to make the decision to marry her. All that he had given up to be with her. She just hoped she was worth it.

"Come on, let's get some rum and take off to the cave," Jerry said.

"Sounds good," Evans replied before tearing his gaze away from the sea.

# Chapter 2

Once they were inside the cave, each man found a seat and a bottle of rum. They were all laughing and carrying on when Evans's father found them, with Jim right behind him.

"Evans, I need you to go with Jim to get his load off his ship. It's damaged and can't sail. I need it delivered now."

"How? My crew just left," Evans said, feeling as though he were drunk.

"That isn't a problem; I'll be your first mate," Jerry said as he stood up.

"I'll be the second," Ray said.

"Count me in!" Rod added.

"And you have me, Cousin," Jim said. "I'll find a few local men, along with some of Jerry's and Ray's men. We can do this. What do you say?"

"Oh hell, when do we leave?" Evans asked as he looked at them.

"In the morning," his father replied. Then he left them all to get ready.

"Bre is going to kill you," Rod said.

"No, knowing her, she'll go, too," Ray said, laughing.

"That's it! You can take her and her family along. Tell them it's a chance to get some things she wanted for the house," Jim said as he took the bottle from Evans.

"Guys, she isn't like that," Evans said to them. "She'll be fine with it."

"I bet you Ray is right, she'll want to go," Jerry said to him.

"That is true," Evans said with a smile.

They sat around for a few more hours, laughing and getting drunk. Then Evans excused himself so he could go home to Bre. He missed and needed her.

He walked into their bedroom to find her standing on the balcony, her long blond hair gently blowing in the wind. She wore one of his white dress shirts, which she typically slept in, and it was moving just enough to hug her curves. Moments like this confirmed for him that he had made the right choice. He couldn't imagine a world without Bre at his side.

Hearing his footsteps, she turned and smiled. He stayed silent as he moved across the room to her, finally wrapping her in his arms and beginning to kiss her.

Minutes later, she came up for air. After she'd caught her breath, she smiled. "You know, you don't have to seduce me. I already know about the trip. In fact, it was my idea. I thought it would make you feel better."

"This was all you?" he asked, looking into her eyes.

"Yes. They were trying to figure out how to get the load delivered, so I said you should do it. I knew your family wouldn't let you go alone."

"Some plan," he said, "but I like it. So are you going with me?"

"Well, I thought—" Before she could finish her thought, he picked her up, carrying her to the bed.

"Princess, I'll put it this way: It's not open for discussion. You're going, too."

"But what about the baby?"

"We'll take him with us. Your parents can help out; we'll have fun. It will give you a chance to pick up some things you wanted for the house."

"Okay," she said with a smile, and then leaned into his kisses.

The next morning, they were down at the docks getting the ship ready to sail when Evans's father walked over. "What's this?"

"We're getting ready," Bre answered.

"Please tell me you're not going with them."

"I am—why?"

"You've never sailed with the likes of them before. I'm afraid they'll scare you for life, or worse," he said with a worried look.

"It can't be as bad as *The Nitingale*'s crew."

"Yes, it can," he quickly said. "Evans, why are you doing this to her?"

"What?" He looked over to his dad.

"Taking her with the likes of all of you."

"She'll be fine, Uncle. Stop worrying. We'll be on our best behavior," Ray said.

"The last time all of you was on one ship, it was bad—very bad. That's why we separated you. Don't you remember? Because I sure do; it cost a fortune to fix."

Bre stared wide-eyed at Darrell, she opened her mouth slightly as she looked at Evans, who gave her a devilish smile. She knew then that Darrell was right: She was in trouble with them.

"Stop worrying, Dad; we're older now."

His father watched two crates of rum being loaded onto the ship, along with a small wooden cradle. "Oh hell," was all he said before walking off.

As they set weigh, Bre watched the cousins work to get the ship out to sea. She was impressed while watching them; they did things differently than the crew she was used to. Shifting her gaze, she watched her brothers work with the same amount of amazement. They hadn't forgotten how to do it, and Austin in particular took to it fast.

Her home disappeared into the distance. This was the first time she'd left her beautiful island since she'd been brought there. She hadn't realized how quickly she'd become homesick.

Walking toward the back of the ship with her baby in her arms, she allowed her mind to wander to Evans and the nightly walks they shared. She pulled baby Evans to her tightly and whispered in his ear, "This is where your parents fell in love. Things are different now, little one. Back then, I only wished to win your father's heart; now I am his wife, holding his son, on his mighty, beloved ship." She smiled and kissed him on the head.

Bre's mother walked up. "Here, let me take him for a while," she said as she reached for the baby.

"Thank you." Bre saw her husband was busy laughing and drinking with his cousins, so she decided to walk around.

She had forgotten how it felt to be on the sea. She had missed the gentle rocking of the boat and the consistent breeze. The smell and taste of salt water on her lips. That once the ship was far enough from port, the only sounds were the waves crashing on the ship and the snap of the sails. The birds could only be heard birds if the ship was near port or land. The sounds of the men working and laughing brought back all kinds of memories. Oh, how she'd missed it! She understood why Evans loved the sea so much, and she still didn't understand how he would be able to walk away from it, even for her.

The sun was starting to set. This was her favorite time. She loved looking to the west and watching while the sun set the water on fire as it went down. The sky was full of orange, red, yellow, pink, and dark gray-blue; if she looked to the east, she saw the dark blue of night, with stars starting to shine brightly.

"Hate to disturb you, my love, but I think you have a sleepy little boy," Elizabeth said as she handed the baby to Bre.

"Thank you. I'll go lay him down." She headed for her room. After opening the doors, she smiled and walked the baby to his cradle. She sat in the chair beside the bed and looked over at the desk.

She remembered pointing the gun at Evans. She was so thankful now that it had been empty, but when it happened, she'd been so mad she hadn't cared it wasn't loaded. Bre's eyes dropped and caught on the faint stain still showing on the rug from that man's blood—the man who'd tried to have his way with her. She was thankful that Evans had come to her rescue when he had. The thoughts of what that man could have done still haunted her.

Glancing at the bed, Bre thought back to when Evans had taken care of her after she'd made herself sick just to get time with him. How afterward she would wake to find his glass lying on the table. How he'd sit in the same chair she now occupied, watching her sleep. *Some things never change*, she thought.

She got up and walked to the windows. Cliff had done a nice job repairing them after the hurricane had knocked them out. She remembered how she had struggled to reach Evans and tied herself to him, fighting out the storm at his side. This ship—this room—was full of memories of their love, the good and the bad.

Evans's cup rolled across the desk's surface. She was afraid the noise would wake the baby, so she picked it up and opened the desk drawer, where she intended to place it. She looked down and found her silk ties lying there. She smiled at them, then noticed a dried rose lying among the brightly colored fabric. She knew it had at one time been white, even if it was now a deep yellowish-brown color. She noticed a dark brown stain on it and shivered, remembering how they'd all been covered in blood. Then she spotted the letter she'd written to Evans, and she smiled, closed the drawer, and laid his cup back on the desk. She didn't want to disturb his treasures of their love. She felt as if she were smiling all over as she stood and headed for the door. She realized that no matter what hold the sea had on her husband, hers was stronger. She left the room to find her love and tell him goodnight.

Pike, Zack, Austin, and Brandon were wrestling around with Jim, Ray, and Rod. Evans and Jerry were talking about life. Her parents were walking around, enjoying the night air.

Bre was pleased that baby Evans took to the ship well. The rocking of the ship put him sound to sleep fast. She knew this would be different than last time. This time she wouldn't be able to spend the nights with her husband. She'd need to sleep when the baby did; that way she could be rested enough to take care of him.

She walked to her favorite spot on the back of the ship and leaned over the railing to enjoy the sea splashing on her face. She just about jumped in when Evans walked up behind her.

He reached out to catch her, starting to laugh. "Already jumping ship after the first night? Has it really been that bad?"

"No," she said as she turned around to face him.

"Just checking," he said with a laugh. "So what is my beautiful princess up to?"

"Just enjoying the night before I have to turn in."

"Oh, may I join my lovely wife?"

"I thought you'd never ask," she said, blushing.

"This is the first time we've been on this ship as husband and wife. The things I could do to you," he said with a scheming grin.

She took his hand and led him to their quarters. "I found my silk ties," she said, turning red.

He just smiled as he spun her around to see her eyes. "Going through my stuff, princess?"

"No, just moving something around. We have a lot of memories in this little room he said, looking around.

"Aye, that we do. Can I kiss you now, or do I have to wait until we've gone down memory lane?" He didn't wait for an answer, kissing her neck and working his way up to whisper in her ear, "I would love to make love to my wife now."

"Oh, Captain Evans," she said with a giggle, then gave in to his kisses.

The next morning, Bre woke up alone in her bed. She noticed Evans standing by the window with their baby in his arms. She lay there for a few minutes, watching them, loving the sight of them looking out the window. Then it hit her: She would miss this if he didn't change his mind and stay on the sea. She had to make him see that they could do it together as a family.

"What is it about this ship?" she whispered to herself.

She climbed out of bed and walked to her husband and baby. "Good morning, my captain," she said as she placed her arms around him.

"Mommy's up," he said, bouncing the baby in his arms. He turned to face his wife, leaned down, and gave her a soft kiss. "How did you sleep, my love?"

"Like old times." She smiled at him.

"I think I'll get Cliff to make a veranda here. I know we'd enjoy that." Thoughts of her standing in the moonlight on their balcony ran through his mind.

"So that means you've decided to stay on the sea?" she asked with a smile.

"No, but I can see me taking you out on romantic moonlit sails."

"Evans—" she began, but he stopped her.

"I am where I belong. I don't want to hear another word about it."

She looked around, then back to him. "Have you forgotten how many fights we've had right here in this room? One more isn't going to make a difference."

"Aye, I also remember you tried to shot me once," Evans said, trying to get her to drop the conversation.

"Well, lucky for us, it wasn't loaded."

"That's not the point, princess. Here," he said, handing their son to her. "I need to check on everything. I love you," he said as he reached and softly kissed her; then he leaned over and kissed the top of their son's head. He left before anything else could be said.

Later that day, Bre was playing with the baby when she looked over to her mother and asked, "Can you keep your eye on him for a few minutes? I want to go and check on everything."

"Sure," she said as she laid her book down. "Is something wrong?"

"No, just need some fresh air and want to see my husband's smiling face. He loves this so much."

"I can see that. So do your brothers, and that scares me a little."

"There's no safer place for them, as long as they're at Evans's side."

Walking out of the room, Bre saw Zack and Pike at the helm. She looked for Evans but didn't see him. A moment later, she realized that her father was standing there with them. His hands were actually holding the wheel.

Bre watched for a few minutes. Her father was laughing, and smiling at everything. She tried to remember the last time he'd looked that free. She smiled and went on to find her husband.

She found him down below with Jerry, Jim, Ray, and Rod. They were all drinking and carrying on. Just then, Brandon came out from one of the holds carrying an arm full of rum.

Once he saw her, he looked at the bottles and then back at Bre. Acting fast, he handed each man a bottle and said if they needed him for anything else to just yell. Then he tried to hurry out of the way, but Bre moved into his path.

"What's going on down here?" she asked, glaring at them.

"Just some drinking, and teaching Brandon how to hold his rum," Evans said with a smile.

She looked over at Brandon, whose head was ducked down.

"Chicken," one of them called out.

"Are you going to tell?" Brandon asked her.

"No," she said, "but I do want to know why you have Pike, Zack, and my father at the wheel. And where's Austin?"

"He's in the crow's nest, and relax—they can't hurt nothing. It's only water and all they have to do is head due east," Ray said.

"This is my father we're talking about. He might be good at a lot of things, but he is an accident looking for a place to happen."

"You're selling him short, Bre," Jerry said.

"No I'm not. Remember the small boat?" she said to Evans.

"Yeah, but he just didn't know there was rocks that way."

"*You* didn't know there was rocks that way until he found them. He's sort of like Brandon, my love."

"What?" Jerry asked as he looked at Evans, then back to Bre. "You have to tell me this one!" He busted out in laughter.

"Aye," the men all cried out, trying to hide their laughter.

"Okay," Evans said to them. "Would you like to tell it?" he asked his pretty wife.

"No, I'll let you." She glared at him. She was mad, but happy at the same time.

"Well, he was taking the small boat to the big island. Apparently there's a group of rocks between the two along the northeast side. He hit them head-on and got the boat stuck in the middle," Evans said with a laugh.

Brandon spoke up. "Oh, that's not the best part."

"Aye," Evans said after taking another sip of rum. "See, the tide was low at the time, so that could've played a part in this. Anyway, we noticed they hadn't returned and it was getting late. So me and a few others went to find them, and we found them just in time, too." He busted out in laughter. "They was trying to swim to the big island."

"Who was?" Ray asked.

"Brandon, Hoss, and my father," Bre said with a smile. "I thought Hoss was going to kill them, and Evans."

"Aye, he's still mad over that. He makes it sound worse than it is every time he tells it. Claims sharks was circling them," Evans said.

"Man, I hate I missed that one," Ray said with a chuckle.

"Evans," Bre said once they'd stopped laughing. "What are you going to do about my father?"

"Fine, I'll go and take over. Will that make you happy?" Rod asked, then got up and left them in Bre's line of fire. He stopped beside Bre, turned back around, took Evans bottle of rum from him, and whispered this is worse than being at home." Then he went up the steps.

No, that is a chicken, Jerry said as he busted out into laughter. Sharks circling them busted out into laughter again.

Bre smiled and went back up top, hoping that all this would help him see that this is where he need's to be.

Later that night, Bre went to find her husband to tell him good night. She walked around the ship for a little while enjoying the night air. Then she saw all of the men setting around some crates. She walked toward them, up beside her husband.

"Hello, princess," Evans said as he pulled her into his lap.

"We're listening to stories of when they was all together sailing." Pike spoke up as he looked over at her.

"That sounds nice." She smiled at him. It was just what she wanted, for. She wanted Evans to remember all the good times.

"Who's next?" Rod asked as he looked around the men.

"Ill go," Jerry spoke up. "This one's my favorite time."

All then men smiled at Jerry, and the boys moved in closer and Evans just gave him a warning glance.

Bre could feel Evans tighten up under her. She looked at him and noticed the look he was gave Jerry. "What's wrong?"

"Nothing. Let's go for a walk."

"What's wrong?" She looked back at Jerry. Then she realized that the story he was about to tell was one that Evans didn't want her to hear. "I'd like to hear the story," she said.

"Fine, but don't hold it against me, and remember I did have a past before I met you princess." Evans forced a smile, then nodded Jerry to go on with his story.

"It was any other normal time. We was out having fun, doing our job. We stopped at Orcola for a night of overdue rest. We did like we always did, headed straight to the Sandhopper. Well, I don't have to tell you all what we did in there.

"The next morning, we finally sobered up and couldn't find Evans anywhere. So we begin to look for him. We went through all the rooms. . . ." He stopped for a minute as if remembering a certain woman.

Rod spoke up. "Aye, that was a good time,"

"Back to the story," Bre said to them.

"Well," he said with a laugh. "We couldn't find Evans nowhere. So after searching the Sandhopper top to bottom, and no sign of him, we went outside to look for him. There wasn't many places to look—only four buildings: the Sandhopper, the General Store, the bank, and the inn. We didn't find him in any of them, so we went toward *The Reeper* to search for him.

"To our surprise, we found him on the docks, in a trance. He was staring at his one and only true love. She was prefect in every way."

Evans could feel Bre tighten up, but she wasn't saying anything.

"She was a piece of art," Ray spoke up.

"Like an angel," Rod chimed in.

"Guys, she wasn't all that," Jim said, laughing, "but then again, she did steal his heart—something I never thought could happen."

"Come on, princess, let's go to bed," Evans said as he placed his hand on hers.

She had fire in her eyes. "Not until I hear all about this female that stole your heart."

All the men, but Evans busted out into laughter. Evans looked at her a smiled as he placed a piece of her hair behind her ear. "Princess you are the female that stole my heart."

"Evans," she said with a warning glance that told him not to lie to her.

"Let's go, this is just a story from the past that they're making sound worse than it is."

"I'd like to hear the rest," she said to him.

"Okay, but I warn you its not what you thinking." Then he kissed her softly on her lips. "Back to you, Jerry," Evans said to him.

"I walked over to him, and asked if he was alright. After a few minutes, he looked at me and smiled. 'I have to have her,' he said. 'She' is perfect.'

"I told him, 'We can't take her,' and as the others join us. They all tried their best into get Evans on the ship, but he wasn't not going to leave with out his love. So we hatched out a plan to steal her."

"You mean kidnap her," Bre snorted.

"No, steal her," Jerry said with a smile.

Bre folded her arms and held herself on Evans knee, remembering when they took her. This wasn't the first time they did it. He had kidnapped another girl. She wondered what ever happened to her.

"So we got on *The Reeper* and pulled away from the dock closer to his love. He ordered the men to board the ship, but not harm it."

Bre looked with eyes as wide as ever. Then she turned to Evans. "He is talking about the time you took this ship, not a female. You allowed me to believe...."

"No, you assumed, I tried to warn you it wasn't what you thought my love." Evans said as he busted into laughter.

"Why, you!" She hit him, as she busted out into laughter.

"You do know that jealous isn't your strong suit princess."

"Shut up," she said as she smiled at him. "I could remind you of that too."

"Shh!" Zack said to them. "We want to hear the rest of the story."

"We already know that he got the ship. Look we are on it!" Brandon said.

"Boys," Bre's father said, "I'd like to hear the rest too, but we can't with you two fighting!" He laughed.

Jerry went on with the story, and Evans took his wife's hand and led her toward their room.

# Chapter 3

They reached the island, and Pike, Zack, Austin, and Brandon helped Evans and the crew get the ship ready to dock. Bre was preparing everything to take her parents into the small town. She kissed Evans and told him they'd meet him later in front of the inn.

"Do you have your gun? What about your dagger?" he asked, looking her over.

"Yes, the gun is here," she said as she tapped her skirt pocket, "and the dagger is on me." She smiled, blushing.

"That's my girl," he said with a smile as he leaned in to kiss her again. "Be careful. I'll be that way soon." He kissed her one more time.

"I will," she said and walked to her parents. They headed for the little town, which wasn't far from the docks. As she studied the town, she realized that it reminded her of Charles Towne. The smell was awful, and filth lined the streets. The roads were muddy, as were the wooden sidewalks. It was nothing like the big island she'd become accustomed to.

On her island, once you stepped off the boat, you'd smell exotic flowers mixed with the aroma of whatever the locals were fixing for dinner. It was clean, the stone sidewalks stayed swept, and the roads were never *this* muddy, even after a hard rain. The buildings were vibrant and colorful; here, they were just faded wood with mud slung over them.

She was trying not to breathe too much, for every time the smell hit her, she'd feel sick to her stomach. The stench was so bad that she knew it wouldn't leave her until she took a bath.

They finally arrived at the store her mother wanted to explore. Bre heard fussing taking place across the street and turned to investigate.

It was a tall man who was looking down at a boy. Standing behind the pair were six other men and a young girl. The man with his back to Bre was short and fat. He wore a hat that looked funny even for a man's hat. It was full-brimmed and bright blue with what looked to be a peacock feather pinned to the side. He was dressed in a matching blue velvet suit. His pants came past his knees, and he wore white stockings with dark blue, heeled dress shoes. After seeing Evans and his crew for the past couple of years, Bre couldn't help but stare at the man's outlandish attire.

Just then the short man, pushed the young boy, who stumbled into the girl, causing her to fall. Bre ran across the street in time to save her from being run over by a wagon wheel.

"Are you okay?" Bre asked the young girl as she tried to brush the mud off her torn dress.

She appeared to be only a child, and yet she looked older both in her actions and eyes. She struck Bre as a helpless child who needed love and nourishment. She wondered what kind of life anyone could have in this place but was brought out of her thoughts when she heard a man talking to her.

"She's fine, now get on with your business. We're busy here," the man in the bright blue suit said.

Bre turned to face him. "I don't recall asking you for anything, sir. So if you'll excuse me, I'd like to hear it from this young lady before I go." Then she turned back to the girl. "Are you okay?"

"I'll be fine. Thank you for your help."

"Now you heard, so go," he said. "We have business to attend to. I won't tell you again."

Just then Bre saw Evans and Jerry heading her way. She smiled at the fat man and told him no.

"No?" he said "I will—"

"You'll what?" Evans said from behind him. "If you touch one hair on my wife's head, I will kill you, Fat Louie." The thought of the fat bastard laying a hand on his wife, let alone talking to her like he had, was enough to set Evans over the edge. He grabbed Fat Louie, spun him around, and punched him in the mouth, causing everyone standing there jump back out of his way.

Holding his mouth, he got up off the ground, starting to cuss. Once he turned around, he froze and then took a few steps backward when he saw Evans. "I thought you had retired."

Bre couldn't help but begin laughing after seeing him roll around in the mud. She pulled herself together when Evans turned his cold stare her way. Without taking his eyes off Bre, he responded to Fat Louie, "Never. Just took some time off. So what was that you was saying to my wife?"

"Nothing. I was just thanking her for helping Mrs. Nunn. That was all. Really, there's nothing here for you to be concerned about."

"Well, if it's okay with you, I'll ask this young boy."

"Fine," he said as he turned to give the boy a warning glance.

"Who do you sail for?" Evans asked the boy.

"I am currently unemployed," the boy said.

"How come?"

"I'm not sure. We was on our way to the docks when he stopped us," he said, gesturing to Fat Louie.

"What does he want?"

Mrs. Nunn who was hiding behind Bre spoke up. "He wants more of the money. So we can't sail unless we agree to it."

"What money?" Evans asked.

"He wants more. He normally gets 30 percent, but now he wants 60 percent," Nunn answered.

"What's your name, son?" Evans asked him.

"They call me Nunn. This is Swamp Fox, and this is Brittany. The rest of them is Jared, Big Jon, Ray, Linds, and Jacob."

"Nice to meet you. They call me Captain Evans." He turned to Fat Louie. "Let me get this straight: Since they're just kids you thought you could make them agree to this. What were you going to do? Take the girl so they had no choice but to agree, or maybe kill one of them to send a message?"

"This doesn't concern you. Besides, it looks as if you're short-handed," he said with a laugh, looking behind Evans at Jerry and the three young boys.

"I don't need anyone else to whip you," Evans snapped, "but if it makes you feel more important, I can get the rest of my crew by my side."

"Like you could really do that. I see no weapons on you, and your crew passed by here a few days ago. Do you know how upsetting that is? Here you are, this once-mighty captain who's now weak. It looks as if the rumors are true. You did lose your mind when you found that young pretty thing." he said as he pointed to Bre.

Evans gave Bre a warning glance as Fat Louie moved closer to her. She placed her hand into her pocket and gripped the gun so all she had to do was fire it through her skirt if she needed to.

"Aye, that crew has split. But I wasn't talking about them. I was talking about my original crew. Hell's crew," Evans spit, his eyes flashing with anger.

Before anything else could happen, Mark yelled out to Evans, "I see that no matter where you go, you need my help!"

"Not this time; I plan to kill him. Just stay out of the way," Evans said without diverting his eyes from Fat Louie.

Ray, Jim, and Rod came around the corner. "We got this covered, but if you like, we'll leave you some," Ray said. "Here—you left these behind." He tossed Evans's his belt, that had his sword, and two pistols rolled up in it, to him.

Fat Louie knew he was out-skilled and that they could each kill five or more of his men without breaking a sweat. Sure, he had the men, but he didn't want to lose them—not like that. So he looked at Evans and said, "I'll tell you what. I'll give you these boys and some useful information—as long as you leave my island at once. All of you."

"What boys?" Evans asked.

"Nunn and his crew, along with their families."

"That's not up to you or me. That's up to them," Evans said.

Nunn immediately stepped forward. "We would be honored. Give us an hour and we'll be on your ship." Without waiting for a reply, he disappeared with his men to get their things.

"Now what was that information you had?"

"I heard there's a ship coming off the Ivory Coast. It's called *The Phoenix*. It will be loaded down with ivory and gold. It's heading to the Americas. I know of a ship that will be waiting for it in the Sargasso Sea. They plan to take the treasure and sink the ship."

Evans held his hands in tight fists at his side. "Are you sure about this?"

"Aye, it's been the talk of the town for days."

"Is this your doing?" Jerry asked him.

"No, I have nothing to do with this. I thought about it, but it wasn't worth my time," he said with a smile.

"If you're lying to me, I promise you I will come back here and kill you. Even if it means I have to burn this town to the ground to find you."

"I'm not, and why does it mean so much to you anyway?"

"That is my ship, but you already knew that, didn't you?" he said in a low growl.

Fat Louie busted out in laughter. "What a small world."

In return, Evans punched him in the mouth again. This time he stood over him, keeping him from standing. "I keep my word, and don't ever forget it."

Fat Louie's men moved in closer. Evans gave them a warning look. "I don't think this is really what your men want to do," he said as he moved to let the bleeding man get up.

Fat Louie yelled for his men to stop, ordered them to leave, went with them, and did so in a hurry.

Evans called, "I'll finish this one way or another. I'm a man of my word.!"

But Fat Louie never turned around. He just kept walking, waving at some of the people standing on the streets, who were watching him run from a fight with Evans and his crew.

Evans turn to his cousins. "Well, it looks like we're getting bloody. Are you all ready?"

They all said aye at the same time.

Bre stared at him blankly. "What about the baby, my parents?" she said in a whisper.

Evans pulled her to him. "Don't worry." He held her close and turned to Mark, who was standing nearby. "Can you help?"

"Yes, I'm going by that island of yours you call Hell anyway, so I can drop them off. Who am I taking?"

"My son, my parents, and my boys. The women who are coming with the new men, and my wife."

"We're not going, Evans," Zack said in a hurry. Brandon, Austin, and Pike nodded in agreement.

"This is not the time for your stubbornness," Evans said. "Let's get back to the boat; then we can discuss this."

Evans didn't say much as they walked back to the ship. His mind was all over the place. This was his fault, and he knew it. Along with making it right, he knew what he had to do, and he prayed that he'd get there in time to stop it.

He worried about leaving his wife and son. This was why he hadn't wanted to return to the sea. If something happened to him, where would they be? At the same time, he worried about his men. If he couldn't get to Steven in time, the men would perish, and where would that leave their families?

He had never thought about the collateral damage before. He'd always been focused only on the fight at hand. Now his focus was on surviving and bringing the men home to their families alive.

He was putting too many people's lives at stake by going to Steven's and his crew rescue. His father would never get over such a loss if they never returned. Evans had every captain his father had with the exception of Hoss.

Then Evans thought about him and Hoss talking about that feeling that something was wrong about them splitting up.

Evans picked up a few boys, realizing they didn't know the first thing about fighting. They were fishermen, and he'd have bet good money that they'd never been in a battle or seen the man on the right or left of them fall.

He just hoped he could get there in time. It didn't sit well with him that he was at fault. He put his friends, the men he loved as family, into harm's way. He should have listen to his gut, and stayed out for one more season. Instead he'd listened to his heart and had returned to the sea, deciding it was the best thing for his wife and son.

Evans knew he had to fix this. He just prayed that they'd all forgive him, especially if he didn't get there in time. That thought drove his anger into full force. He wanted to kill everyone who had a hand in the planned siege of *The Phoenix*. He was convinced that Fat Louie knew more then he'd admitted. He wished he had time to blow the town to dust, but lucky for them, he didn't have that kind of time on his hands.

At the dock, the women were loading their things onto *The Monte Carlo*. Bre was helping her parents with the baby's things while trying to convince her mother that the boys would be safe with Evans. They had to grow up some time, despite how their mother felt about it. This was the life they had chosen for themselves.

Zack and the boys still said they were going with Evans, and Bre refused to go back without her husband. She was trying to convince Evans that she would be fine and that she could help.

Finally Mark looked at Evans and spoke before he could again tell Bre no. "This bunch reminds me of the first time I took you and them cutthroats you have with you now. No one thought any of you all was ready, but you was. Just as they are. You know it as well as anyone, Evans. They'll back you 100 percent, just as you did me, and that wife of yours—she would kill the *world* for you if she had to for you. So take them. Besides, you're the best I've ever seen on these seas. Who better to teach them and get them ready than you and them misfits with you?"

"Fine, they can go," Evans said, looking them over. Then he turned to Bre. "*You* are going with Mark and your parents."

"No I'm not."

"Yes," he said as he looked into her eyes. "You need to be home with our son. What if something happens out there? Who would take care of him?" He pointed to his baby, who was being held by Bre's mother.

"Oh no, you are not pulling that with me. We will be fine and home before he even misses us. Now go over there and kiss him goodbye. Then we're off to save Steven."

She then turned to her parents. "We'll be back soon. Take care of him until we return, and I'll take care of my brothers. I bet that when we get back, you won't recognize them."

"Just as you will not yours," Bre's mother replied with a hug. "Please take care of them, and yourself. I promise to do all I can to keep your baby safe." Then she got onto the ship, so she could let her fear, and tears flow freely. She was doing her best to stay strong for her daughter.

Bre's father walked over to her. "I love you." He turned to Evans. "Take care of my children," he said, and then he joined his wife on the ship.

"Got room for one more?" Marks brother Tim asked Evans.

"Aye," he said with a wondering look.

Tim turned to his brother. "I think it would be best if I go with them to help."

Mark laughed. "That's fine, I'll catch up to you later." He gave his brother a hug, gave Evans one, and then walked to his ship.

Evans started giving the crew orders to set weigh. Bre stood at the helm as she watched her family head home. She said a short, silent prayer that they'd reach Steven in time and that they'd make it home safe, back to her baby.

# Chapter 4

**B**re kept to herself for the rest of the night. She knew Evans was mad at her, but she also knew he would be fine after some time alone at the helm. Jerry was teaching Zack some gun techniques, and Jim taught Brandon what he needed to know about sword-fighting. Ray taught Pike about hand-to-hand combat, and Rod showed Austin the finer points of knife-throwing.

After they felt they had taught them all they could, they went down to the weapons hold to equip the novices with weapons and proper clothes.

When they came back up, Evans and Bre was both taken back: They were It wasn't the same four boys who'd gone down. Now they were dressed to fight and had the look of true pirates. Her brothers were now men, whether anyone liked it or not.

Over the next few days, the men told the boys what to expect, what to watch out for, and when to make their moves.

They had been on the sea for over a week now, without any sitings of any ships. Evans and Bre were in their chambers looking at the charts, mapping out the route that Steven should have taken and the route he should be on for the return.

"Well, we can count on him wasting a day in town, so that's a day there," Bre said.

"Right, and if our calculations are correct, then we're three days from him, maybe four."

"Let's just hope we're right, and he kept up with his old games. If he left on time, we might be too late." The thought made her shiver.

"Steven's known for his mischief. Unlike Hoss, who's like me: Get in and back out as fast as you can," Evans said.

"Wait, wasn't Hoss going this way?" She pointed to the map.

"Yes," he said, leaning to look closer. "That means we should see his ship in the horizon sometime in the morning, if not sooner. If we can get Hoss, then we can both get to Steven in time."

Just then a call from the helm made them jump. "A ship on the horizon! It has a CP Trading Company flag flying."

Evans and Bre both ran to the helm. Jerry looked at Bre with a cocked eyebrow. This was the first time they'd all seen her out of her normal attire. Now she was dressed to fight. She had on a pair of form-fitting pants and boots that reached her knees. Her blouse was loose but not so baggy that she'd get hung up on it. Her belt held her guns and her sword, and a rifle was slung across her back. She looked different, yet it suited her.

"Can you tell whose ship it is?" Evans yelled to the crow's nest.

"It's *The Sphinx*!" Austin yelled down. "It's Pa," he said, this time louder.

"Thank God," Evans said, smiling for the first time since he'd heard that Steven was in trouble.

"How are we going to get his attention? It's almost dark; if we don't do something now, he'll sail past us," Tim said.

"Load a cannon fire in his direction. It will get his attention. Then they'll see it's us," Jerry said with a smile.

"What if it hits him?" Bre asked. "Our cannons are able to reach that distance."

"We won't put a cannonball in it if it makes you feel better," Rod said with a smile as he prepared the cannon to fire.

"No, put one in and aim for the front. Make sure you miss it by a foot or two," Evans said. "We want to make sure we get his attention."

As they fired, they saw Hoss and Dean on the helm.

They were talking about making good time when the cannonball hit the water in front of them, splashing them.

"Who's in the crow's nest?" Hoss said in anger. "I want to know what damn idiot let this happen." Then he yelled, "Men, to your stations! We are getting ready for battle."

Dean looked at Hoss. "There's only one ship that can reach that far."

"Yes, but she's at home and part of her crew is here." He yelled, "Can you see what ship she is?"

"She's hosting her colors now," Darron called out, looking through his spyglass. Then he quickly turned to Hoss. "She is no longer in berth."

"What do you mean?" Hoss took the spyglass.

"It's *The Nitingale*."

"It's impossible," Hoss said as he looked. "Why would they fire on us unless. . . . Get our ship next to them. Host our colors as well. We're going to have fun yet!"

"Wait!" Ronnie called out. "It might be *The Nitingale*, but what if it's a trap? Someone could've got to her. We would never know until it was too late."

"Stop being stupid," Dean said. "It's Evans."

"Maybe, but what if he's right? Evans doesn't have a crew to sail her," Darron said.

"Stop it. Let's get closer to her. If we see it's not Evans, we'll make the call then," Hoss said. The thought of sinking her made him sick to his stomach.

It was dark by the time they reached *The Nitingale*. Hoss moved his ship closer, just enough to talk but yet not able to cripple him if it a trap.

Hoss!" Evans called out.

"Evans? Hoss yelled back. "What is going on?

Get over here and we can talk instead of yelling back and forth. Evans said to him.

Hoss moved his ship closer so they could tie off to each other. Then he and his right hand men moved over to *The Nitingale*.

Once Hoss stepped foot on the ship, he noticed Jerry, Ray, Jim, Rod, Tim, Pike, Zack, and Austin was all dressed for battle. What's going on?

Just then Bre moved out of the shadows to stand next to Evans. Steven' is in trouble. Was all she said.

Everyone was looking at Bre and the way she was dressed. Hoss just looked at her then back to Evans. First, what's this about Steven. Second what is my son doing here, and third what are all of you doing here.

"It's like this: We told Evans that my ship was damaged. We wanted him to feel good about himself after all of you left. So we cooked up a plan for him. We all stepped in as his crew. Then when we got there to deliver it. We got into it with Fat Louie. He told us that Steven was in trouble, in order to save his own hide. Mark was there; he took the woman and Bre's parents with their son home. We set out sail to find Steven," Jim said.

Evans just looked at him for a moment then Bre. Then he told them that he would deal with them later. "The boys refused to go. I understand how they felt it was like us a long time ago. While we was looking at the charts, we remembered you'd be passing by here. We're glad we got to you before dark, or we would have missed you."

"Did you really have to fire the cannonball?" Hoss asked them.

"I told them not to, but they didn't listen," Bre said with a small smile.

"Why are you dressed like that?" he finally asked her.

"I can't fight in a dress. So this just made sense. It's what I wear to practice in."

"Fine. Austin, I'll deal with you in a minute. For now, what's the plan of action?"

After Evans filled him in, Hoss stayed silent for a moment, just looking at him. "You've gone mad," he finally said. "Your father would kill us if he knew what was going on here. We have every one of his captains in this. If something happens, CP Trading will be destroyed for good."

"Then we just make sure nothing happens," Ray said with a grin.

"We're empty, and you're lighter than Steven's ship. We can count on him messing around town for at least a day, so that puts us at least three days out," Evans said.

"Sounds good to me. Who's behind this attack?" Hoss asked.

"We don't know yet, but I have a feeling it's Fat Louie," Jerry said.

"Talk about feelings," Hoss muttered to Evans.

"Yeah, I know. All this time we thought it was because we was splitting up. I should have trusted it from the get go. Maybe then we wouldn't be in this mess," Evans said.

"How was we to know that the *stupid* one would be the one in trouble I thought the same thing you did, so don't blame yourself," Hoss said.

"Where's Darron? Evans asked before anything else could be said about the feeling they'd both had.

"Darron!" Hoss yelled. "Get over here, Cap needs you."

A few minutes later Darron swung over from *The Sphinx* to *The Nitingale*. What is it, Cap?" he asked as he walked over to them.

Evans handed him a spyglass. "I need you to get to work. I need this to see farther than normal. You're the only one that can do it."

"Let me see what I can do." He took it and began to walk off, then paused. Before he could say anything, Evans butted in, "Yes, your tools are where you left them."

Then Darron disappeared to his work station down below.

Hoss looked over at Austin. Son, it's time we had that talk. Get your ass over there." He pointed to his ship. "Cap, I'll talk to you later. I have something more important to do right now."

"Don't be too hard on him," Bre said with a smile. "He only did what any of us would do. . . ." She paused and looked up at him. "He only did what the rest of us *are* doing. Taking care of family."

Hoss looked at her and slowly smiled before heading over to his ship.

# Chapter 5

They left the ships tied together for the next few days as they traveled. Darron fixed the spyglass for Evans within minutes. Bre watched as everyone prepared for battle. She noticed that everyone on *The Nitingale* worked as one unit. No orders were given, and no one had to ask what to do. They all looked as if they were true hardcore pirates—even her brothers had changed. Their faces made them look older than they were. Hard labor mixed with the sun made them appear tough and worn. She was amazed by it all.

She looked over to Hoss, who was giving orders and telling the men what to do. She was glad to have the noise coming from his ship because the silence emanating from hers would have driven her mad. She knew now why her father-in-law had acted the way he had after finding out they were all sailing together.

They meant business and were looking for a kill—how many and the method used didn't seem to bother them in the least. All they could see, think, smell, hear was blood. It frightened her a little to see her brothers were in that same frame of mind, but she knew in order to survive, they had to be.

They had put Rod up in the crow's nest on *The Nitingale*, and Dean was in the crow's nest on *The Sphinx*. It was only a matter of time before they would find *The Phoenix*.

Sure enough, Steven came into their sights the next morning. They untied the two ships and moved apart to get to *The Phoenix*.

Evans waited until he was within firing distance, then ordered them to open fire on the ship behind Steven's.

After the first cannonball hit the ship behind *The Phoenix*, Steven turned to Glover. "Who's in the crow's nest?"

"It's Mike," he answered. Then they heard three more cannonballs hit the ship behind them.

"Turn around to help. We can't let him sink," Steven ordered.

"I wouldn't do that if I was you, boy," Danny said as he and the others moved in.

"Why not? So help me, if one of you open your mouth about 'that's not what Evans would do,' I'll lock you up in the holds!"

Cliff grabbed the spyglass from Glover and took a look for himself. He just smiled and handed the glass back to Glover. "Do what you want, but I'll take my chances in the brigs before I'll go into battle for someone we don't know." Then he just walked off.

"What are you doing?" Steven asked Cliff.

"I'm going to get my weapons ready. It's just a matter of time before that ship catches us. When it does, I'm jumping ship," he said before walking away.

Steven turned to Glover. "Will you please tell me what's going on?"

"Boy, we all know you're doing your best."

"Yes, but what?"

"We're just inclined to believe that Cap wouldn't want us helping them. He'd want us to help the one doing the firing."

"And what makes you so sure?" Steven said as he took the spyglass.

43

"Because Cap's on the ship that's firing. The one flying *The Nitingale's* true colors."

"Impossible," he said. "She's at home, and half her crew is here while the other half's on *The Sphinx*."

"Maybe so, but that isn't stopping him."

"What is going on?" Steven said as he lifted the spyglass to his eye.

Danny walked over then. "Son, I love you, but you have poor judgment. Glover and I both warned you against telling everything to them men last night. But you didn't listen. It's a trap. They plan to take our load and kill us. We should be glad that Evans is here to help."

"It's *The Sphinx* behind her with her colors flying high. What do you want us to do?" Mike asked Steven.

Jeff walked over and smacked Steven's back. "I told you Evans wouldn't stay home. It's just not in him," he said as he walked away, laughing.

"Fighting stations, men!" Steven yelled. "Once she turns to fire on *The Nitingale*, we turn to fire on them." Just then a shot came over the helm, causing the men to hurry.

Steven kept an eye on them approaching, waiting for his time to turn around. At the right moment, he ordered his men to fire the back cannons.

He watched as Hoss moved to *The Phoenix*'s starboard side while *The Nitingale* moved to the broadside. Finally *The Morning Star* made its decision and began to turn around to fight. Once its broadside faced *The Sphinx*, Hoss ordered his men to fire all eight cannons at once, causing heavy damage to *The Morning Star*'s front. Simultaneously, Evans's men fired all cannons, giving the back side just as much damage.

Once *The Morning Star* was turned around, its crew opened fire on *The Nitingale* and *The Sphinx*, but the damage made was minimal.

Steven had turned around but couldn't get a clean shot with his cannons without firing on Hoss.

Just then, Evans and Hoss got *The Morning Star* between them and opened fire, leaving nothing in their path but a mess. They sailed to Steven and watched *The Morning Star* as it started to sink. There was no evidence of a fight, let alone evidence of it ever being a ship.

Once Hoss and Evans caught up to Steven, they tossed over ropes to tie *The* three ships together. Steven waited until everything was tied before going over to the *Nitingale*. Hoss was already on Steven's ship, heading toward Evans. He didn't even take time to speak to Steven; he knew that making him wait would kill him. Once they were all on *The Nitingale*, Steven noticed that it wasn't just Evans on the ship, but also Jerry, Jim, Ray, and Rod.

Steven stood there for a few minutes, shaking his head. Then he looked up at Evans with a smile. "What is this? I thought we were on the up and up. Then out of nowhere you show up with the rest of the cutthroats—and Hoss. I thought you retired."

"I did," Evans said. "Things happened that I had to take care of, and that includes you."

"Funny, here I thought you was attacking *The Morning Star* because you wanted their haul. I would've never thought they were after me. I guess you really can't trust pirates."

"What?" Hoss couldn't believe what he'd just heard.

It doesn't matter. The only thing that does is that he learned something this time. Because next time we might not be around," Evans said to Steven, as if he were scolding a child.

"Well, what are we going to do about this?" Hoss asked Evans.

"All right, we know Fat Louie had something to do with this. How else would he have known about the load. We know they befriended Steven in some way, for him to want to protect them. What are we missing?"

"That *The Morning Star* is one of his ships," Nunn said from the back of the crowd.

"No, they sailed for a trading company out of Virginia," Steven said in a hurry.

"No, I would know. I worked for Fat Louie for a while, and that's one of his ships. He was behind this the whole time," Nunn said to them.

"Okay, Steven, you take your load on to be delivered. Hoss will escort you to make sure this doesn't happen again. We'll set out to get the bastard once and for all," Evans said.

"Like hell! Hoss said. "Look, I' am going with you. I done have blood on the brain and I wont be happy until I get more of it.

Stop it!" Steven said to them. "He was after me, so I'm going, too. I deserve to have fun. Besides, aren't three ships better than one?"

"Guys, you're not thinking clear," Jim said from behind them. "He knows that we know. He knew as soon as we left that we'd find out it was him. So that means he's on the run."

"That's right. So if we went after him, he wouldn't be there. We need to find out where he's hiding, then go after him," Ray added.

"Let's all just sit back and think. Make out a plan, then go after him when he doesn't think we're after him anymore. Between the five of us, surely we can hear something in a tavern or a port."

"Make that six," Bre said, stepping up.

"What?" Evans asked her.

"Look, as long as the word is out that you're retired, this will keep happening. So if *The Nitingale* is out and about, our ships are safe from attack."

"She's right, Evans," Darron said from behind him.

"Okay then, we'll all go. . . . No, that won't work. All right, I'll escort you back as far as my turnoff for Hell. Then Hoss, you see that Steven gets to his port safely. That way we can get these cutthroats back on the sea before Dad has heart failure."

"Cap, I noticed that you're out of most of your food. I'll get you some from *The Sphinx*," Ronnie said. "It wouldn't be much, but maybe Steven has some to spare."

Steven raised an eyebrow to Evans. "Out of food? That's not like you."

"We was only going on a short trip. A week at most. Then we heard about you and we set off without taking time to get supplies."

"I understand. Come with me," Hoss said to Evans. "I have some of Wendy's rum on my boat."

Once they left, the men went back to lying around at ease.

Steven looked over at Bre. "Why are you dressed like that?"

"To save your skinny neck," she said with a smile. "I don't know why, I'm sure it's because they didn't want to turn the sharks against them."

"Funny," he said. Then he looked out at Bre's brothers. "What happened to them?"

"Well, you could say that you made them grow up."

"Me? I had nothing to do with that. When I left they were just kids who'd fall for my jokes."

"Well, in coming after you, they adapted to this life once and for all. They're true men now, or should I say true pirates. They grew up fast."

"So I cause a lot," Steven said as if he were proud of himself.

"You could, but this time I know you was innocent," Bre said before busting out in laughter.

"So who are the new guys?" Steven asked.

"They're some of Fat Louie's men that we picked up on the island. They're good boys. The tall one's name is Nunn. That's Mongo. That one over there is named Ray, them two are Big Jon and Jacob, and this is Linds," she answered. "Who was that on your ship, that my husband's talking to?"

"Oh, that's Jeff. He's an old friend of ours. I found him in Africa and he needed a job, so I gave him one. I knew that Evans wouldn't mind him."

"Oh," she said with a smile as Evans and Jeff came over.

"Princess, I want you to meet Jeff. He's a long time friend I haven't seen in many years."

"Well, now I can see why you was retired," Jeff said with a smile as he turned to Evans.

*Chapter 6*

As the next few days passed, everyone was at ease on the ship. Bre was back to wearing her normal attire and Evans was back to being himself. They were all laughing and cutting up. They were also working, making repairs and doing maintenance that needed to be done.

Evans was talking with the men one morning when he decided that Bre was right: He needed to be out at sea for at least one more season. So they went through the men to put together a good crew for him.

Steven told Evans that he was welcome to whoever on his crew wanted to go with him. Hoss echoed the sentiment, so they gathered all the men for a meeting about the crews.

Glover was the first to speak up. "I don't know about the rest of you, but I'll be his first mate if he'll have me."

"I would be honored," Evans said.

"I'll be the second mate," Dean said before anyone else could.

"He needs someone to repair it, that'll be me. Besides, I told him I was jumping ship once you got close enough," Cliff said in his relaxed way.

Nunn spoke up. "I would like to sail for you."

Then Brandon looked at him. "I will, if you'll have me."

"Well, looks like I have a good crew," Evans said with a smile. Then he turned to Hoss. "How many are you short now?"

"Just one. I need to replace Dean. Who do we have left?"

"Why does he get to go first?" Steven whined.

"You got the new ship, so I get to pick the new crew," Hoss said.

"We have , Ray, Mongo, Big Jon, Linds, and Jacob," Evans said.

"All right then, men, who wants to sail for a man who doesn't take his time in town? Who believes the faster we are on the water, the better life is?"

Jacob raised his hand. "That would be me, sir."

"Your name?"

"Jacob, sir. They call me Jake. I'm a good carpenter."

"Welcome aboard *The Sphinx*, boy."

Evans turned to Steven. "It's your turn."

"Finally," he joked. "I need to replace a few men. Who wants to sail for me? I'm just the opposite of these two. I like to have fun."

Ray, and Mongo spoke up.

"Good! Let's go and get into mischief, men," Steven said to them with a grin.

Evans noticed that two were left. "Big Jon, Linds, why didn't you choose a ship?"

"We'd rather sail for you, but you said you had a full crew, so—"

Evans stopped him. "That doesn't mean anything. Welcome aboard. Next time, you need to speak up." Then he walked away.

Later that day, Evans called his right-hand men to his side for a meeting. "I just wanted to say thank you for stepping up like this. However, this might not be a full-time thing. So if it comes to that, and you want to stay on the seas, I'll understand if any of you chooses to sail for Hoss or Steven."

"Not happening. We could use some downtime as well. We're

sticking with you no matter what. Right, men?" Cliff said. "We know what it's like with out you, and trust me: Where you go, we go."

"Do all of you feel that way?" Evans asked the men, who had circled around him.

"Yes," they all spoke at the same time.

"Well, let's get to work. Who's doing the cooking tonight? For, tonight, we feast!" Evans said.

"I'll go," Brandon said as he disappeared down below to start.

Zack and Pike approached Evans when it was just him standing there. "Can we talk to you for a few minutes?" Pike asked him.

"Yes, what is it boys?"

"We want to sail for you too," Pike said with a small smile.

"Well, I didn't think you'd sail for anyone else. Not yet, anyway," he said as he pulled them into an embrace.

"So we can go with you?" Pike asked, hugging him back.

"Where I go, you go. We're family, and family sticks together."

"I told you so," Zack said to Pike. "Here you thought he was going to leave us at home with Bre."

"You did too," Pike said in a hurry.

"Where is your sister?" Evans asked them both, beginning to look around for her.

"Somewhere. It's a ship; she can't go far," Zack said with a smile.

"She was over there talking to that new girl, Linds," Pike said, pointing.

Evans looked over, but she wasn't there. He excused himself to find his wife. He went to their chambers first, and there she was, piled up and sound asleep.

He stood there watching her for a few minutes. He knew this was the first time she'd slept since they set weigh to find Steven.

Later that night, all the men gathered to eat dinner. Brandon was proud of himself for cooking.

All the men smiled after taking their first bites. Big Jon looked over to Brandon. "How did you learn to cook?"

"This was my first time," Brandon said as he reached for his cup of grog.

"Well, it's perfect no one would have ever known," Big Jon said as he took another bite.

"Think this is better than Ronnie's any night," Glover said, shoving another forkful into his mouth.

# Chapter 7

The next day, all the men were getting ready to cut the ships loose when Dean yelled out, "Three ships on the horizon! They're flying their colors. It's Fat Louie in the lead."

Hoss, Steven, and Evans all yelled orders to their men: "Get ready for battle, men!" "Get the men from the sides and load the cannons!" "Get a move on!"

"Cap," Nunn said, running up to Evans.

"What is it, boy?"

"Our cannons are still up and loaded. I thought he might do something like this."

"I would've never took him to be this stupid," Evans muttered. "Well, in that case, fire the cannons."

"Cap, we're still out of range," Nunn said with a confused look on his face.

"Not for these cannons," Darron said with a smile. "These are *my* cannons—I made them specially for moments like this one."

Bre ran back to her room to change her clothes. She was almost done when Evans hurried into the room to get his weapons. He looked at her and smiled weakly. "I love you, princess. Please be careful and keep safe."

She moved to him and kissed him softly on the lips. "I will, and you do the same."

"Always! I have too much to live for, for once," he said, his smile strengthening. "Ready?"

"As long as I'm with you, yes." The nerves in her stomach were beginning to come into play. She hadn't been in a fight like this in over a year.

She hoped she wouldn't let her husband down.

As they left their chambers, they heard Glover order for the cannons to be fired. He watched through the spyglass as the balls hit *The Neptune*. "We're still not close enough to cause heavy damage—just light. I want this second load to cause damage, so get ready."

This time, they loaded the cannons with anther of Darron's creations. They were like normal cannonballs but had sharp metal spikes protruding from them so they'd cause more damage.

They were all silent as they watched the spiked balls launch across the water, and then they all cheered when the balls hit and caused significant damage to *The Neptune*. They watched as the wood splintered, falling like snow, blanketing the deck of the ship.

Fat Louie muttered under his breath, "Damn Evans and his ship."

Just then his first mate appeared. "I told you we shouldn't have come after them. I tried to tell you that they wasn't just stories. There's something special about his ship."

Fat Louie just looked at him and smiled, then pulled out his pistol and shot him first mate dead. He then turned to his men. "If any other feels as he does, speak now. If not, get back to work."

Then he ordered his cannons to fire, but they were unsuccessful, as he was still too far away to reach *The Nitingale* or the other two ships. After his last round went off, Fat Louie ordered the ship to turn starboard so he could use all twelve cannons to fire nonstop.

Once Evans saw *The Neptune* turning, he ordered for the front cannons to be fired, causing major destruction to Fat Louie's ship's side.

Hoss and Steven watched as the other two ships moved away from *The Neptune*. They weren't sure if the ships were running or moving into a fighting position, so Hoss and Steven moved their ships away from *The Nitingale*, returning to their initial positions. Hoss went after *The North Star* while Steven went after *The Western Star*.

Evans watched as his comrades' ships moved away. He told his men, "Hold straight! We're after Fat Louie."

Bre hollered orders to the men, "Drop the sheets or we'll pass him. We need to slow down!" Just then Bre noticed that Hoss was going after *The North Star*. "Fire the cannons on the portside!"

Jerry turned to her. "We can't do that—the battle is on the starboard side."

"Hoss is on our portside. We need to damage that ship before he gets to it," Bre said.

Jerry looked for himself and then said, "Well, men, you heard her—fire!"

Glover just smiled and looked at Cap. "We taught her well."

"That we did," Evans said, nodding at his princess. Then he looked around at the boys. "Men, we're getting ready to board. Jerry, Jim!" he called out. "Make sure my boys stay next to you. Bre, you take care of our portside. Give them all the hell you can."

"Once we're done here, I'm going to find me a girl like that to kidnap," Jerry said.

Most of the men laughed loudly; the new men looked around, puzzled. Nunn asked Glover what Jerry had meant.

"Boy, that's a story we'll tell on a different day."

Nunn looked at Bre, then over to Evans, and just shook his head. He probably didn't want to know.

Bre ordered the cannons to fire once more, causing heavy damage to the ship Hoss was about to encounter. She turned her attention to *The Western Star*, which was moving closer to Steven. She couldn't reach them yet and waited for the right moment.

Hoss looked at his men. "Get ready, men. We're almost ready to board." He then turned to Ronnie. "Thank God for *The Nitingale*."

"Just tell me this: Are you sure we'll have to fight? By the way things look, Evans will sink her before we even get to board." More rounds of cannonballs peppered the side of *The Morning Star*.

"Fire on the other ship!" Bre yelled as it moved into their line of fire.

The men on *The Nitingale* were dispersed and busy with their own smaller battles. Some were on Fat Louie's ship while some of his men were on *The Nitingale*. Bre tried to hold her position, but it was killing her to not being in the middle of the chaos, by her husband's side.

Just then Bre noticed Jim getting over powered by several of Fat Louie's men. So she picked up her rifle and one of the men in her sights. She steadied herself with the rocking of the ship as she pulled the trigger. Hitting the man in the chest.

Jim never stopped to see who fired; he was simply thankful for it.

Hoss opened fire on *The Morning Star*, causing severe damage. Then he ordered his men to board. "But remember one thing: Leave no one alive!"

Bre ordered for *The Nitingale's* cannons to again fire on *The Western Star*. Once it was heavily peppered by cannonballs, it  to show its starboard side.

"It's running!" one of the hands yelled out.

"Fire, keeping firing until we can't reach it. Bre screamed. She craned her neck again to try to find where Evans was. She reached for her rifle and took aim the man  behind him in the back. He fell landing at Evans feet.

Steven was growing mad by the minute. He wasn't able to catch the cowards on *The Eastern Star* he moved closer to *The Morning Star* to give Hoss a helping hand.

Once Bre noticed that both Hoss and Steven were beginning to board the ship, she ordered the men to fight. "Take nothing and leave nothing but blood!" she called out, then took out her sword and began to fight at Evans's side.

He turned to her and smiled. "It's good to have you back, princess."

"It's good to be back at your side, my love," she replied as they joined the battle.

Evans found a second to turn around and noticed that Hoss and Steven had boarded *The Morning Star*. He knew they would be fine and were more than capable of taking over the ship.

Jim and Jerry were fighting back-to-back, leaving a path of bodies behind them as they worked their way to Evans.

Evans could see Fat Louie standing at the helm, staring back at him smugly. Evans returned his glance and then ordered his men to fire all cannons. He knew *The Nitingale* could withstand the damages from the falling debris. Some likely thought he was mad for this order, but he knew it would make *The Neptune* a death trap.

Bre turned to look at him, and he caught her glance. He gave her a look that said everything was fine and not to worry. Just then, the two ships rocked hard from the blast. Some of *The Neptune*'s mast fell onto *The Nitingale*, causing her to shift.

Ray and Rod had just as many men at their feet as the rest of them. Evans was happy to see that they were safe and taking care of the boys, who had just as many bodies at their feet—more than anyone their age should have.

Evans and Bre both began looking for Brandon but couldn't find him anywhere. Then, all of a sudden, Bre saw him fighting a man who outweighed him thrice over. And one even bigger fellow was coming up behind Brandon. Bre got her gun but remembered she hadn't reloaded it from the last shot. The look on her face made Evans turn without haste. Glover and Jerry both turned with him.

Glover reached for his long rifle to shoot, but Evans snatched it from his hands and fired a shot that took out one of the men. That gave Bre enough time to load her gun; she fired the second round to kill the other man.

Bre and Evans, came to a halt when Brandon fell to his knees. They ran to his side in fear, but he was fine—he was just out of breath. He smiled at them and gasped, "Took you long enough."

Nunn looked around at all the bodies. *The Nitingale*'s deck was stained red from all the blood. He couldn't believe the corpses that were pilled up, and not one of them was from *The Nitingale*'s crew. He'd heard the stories about this ship and her crew, but he hadn't believed them until now. This ship had to have sailed straight from hell, and the crew was working for the devil himself—and now he was one of them.

Bre was different from most of the women Nunn knew. Brittany would have never fought like this, let alone have killed five men. He was amazed by how Bre and Evans had come together and moved as one person.

The men from *The North Star* had given up. They had no more fight in them. Hoss's and Steven's men were disappointed, but they didn't let that stop them from killing the men anyway. They just didn't have to give forth any effort to kill the men.

Finally the fight was almost over, and the only two left standing on *The Neptune* were Fat Louie and his second mate. Evans just looked at him and smiled wickedly—an eerie smile that was unsettling to those around him.

Fat Louie pulled out his pistol and pointed it first at Bre and then back at Evans. He pulled the trigger and the bullet hit Evans in the shoulder. Fat Louie couldn't believe it—Evans had just stood there when he was shot; he didn't even flinch.

Bre ran over to make sure Evans was okay. A small trickle of blood flowed from his arm.

"Don't worry, princess. I'm fine. It's just a scratch. I'll be right back," he said as he smiled at her, never taking his eyes off of Fat Louie. "Glover, come with me," he said and started toward *The Neptune*.

Hoss and Steven had just finished taking over the other ship and turned to watch, as if they'd known exactly when this confrontation would happen.

Evans went straight to Fat Louie, who stood at what was left of his helm. "Looks like there's nothing left of this shabby ship."

"Looks like you're hurt," he returned with a smile.

"No, that's just a scratch. It's nothing compared to what you'll endure in a minute."

"Let me say something before we start. It might help you some. I hate that damn ship of yours, and your crew."

"That's funny; we was thinking the same thing about you," Evans said as he pulled out his sword. "I plan to enjoy this."

Fat Louie turned to look for his second mate, who had just fallen at Glover's feet. He looked back at Evans. "Maybe we can talk about this."

"We're past that," Evans said as he cut his opponent's arm with the first blow of his sword. Then he caught him in his midsection.

Fat Louie backed up, holding his stomach. He looked at Evans and down at the blood that soaked his hand. "They was right. You and your ship are the ghost of the sea."

"No, that's saved for you," Evans said as he gave him one last blow with his shamshir, which took him off of his feet.

As Fat Louie lay there, he looked up at Evans, who stood over him. All he could see was *The Nitingale's* captain moving his lips; he couldn't hear Evans say, "I told you I was going to enjoy this." Then Fat Louie watched as Evans came down on him with vengeance, plunging his sword into his throat.

Evans went back to his ship and yelled to the men, "Take what she has, then blow her belly out."

Jerry handed him a bottle of rum as he walked past.

# Chapter 8

Once the smoke cleared, they could still hear the sounds of *The Neptune* as it sank to the ocean's floor. Ray, Jim, Jerry, and Rod shared a bottle of rum as they watched their destruction disappear beneath the water's surface.

Evans held Bre in his arms and snuggled up to her back. They were talking about how proud they were of Brandon, Zack, and Pike. They had done a fine job, and had proven that they were men, not boys anymore.

*The Nitingale* pulled up beside Hoss and Evans yelled out to them to hurry up, that they didn't have all day to wait to blow her belly out.

"Wait," Steven said. "She doesn't have that much damage."

"Did you not see the portside? Bre caused a lot of damage to it," Cliff said.

"That was Bre?" Steven and Hoss said at the same time.

"Yes, it was," she said to them. "I thought you needed it. The both of you."

Steven and Hoss just looked at each other and then turned to Evans. "What are you going to do with her?" Steven asked.

"Since when do you let a woman give orders?" Hoss said.

"Since she saved the both of you. Next time I'll tell her to let you take care of your own hides."

Just then *The North Star* shifted to her broadside, taking on water. Evans looked at Steven with a smile that all but said, "I told you so."

The men started scurrying around the ship like rats to get what they could off of it before it sank.

Cliff walked over. "It'll be at least a day before she goes completely under. That'll give me enough time to get what I need to fix the three boats. What do you think?"

"Take what men you need for that," Evans said. "Mike, you gather a few and get her sails. We might need them." Then he looked at his family. "Let's go," he said.

"Where?" Hoss asked him.

"We'll give Cliff a helping hand. We can start pulling planks from her good side."

"Great, now we're monkeys too," Steven said as he followed them.

Bre just laughed and began to follow, but her joy turned to anger when Evans told her to stay up top.

"I'm going, too," she said sternly. "If I can fight beside you, then I can surely help pull the planks."

"Fine, but get into one of the cannon holes and we'll hand you the wood. That way you're helping but staying safe."

A little later, Cliff came by and noticed that all the captains were hanging from the side of *The North Star*. They already had half of the ship's planks pulled. Cliff just shook his head and looked down at them. "What's this?"

"We thought we'd help," Jerry said.

"Get your asses back up here where you all belong. I have men to do this," he barked. "I'm just surprised that Bre isn't hanging down there as well!"

Just then Bre popped her head out of a cannon hole. "What was that, Cliff?"

"That's it, I want all of you up here right now," he shouted.

Everyone went back to *The Nitingale* and was sitting around, drinking rum and celebrating their victory, when Bre came over to Evans. "Let's go," she said.

"Right now?" he said with a seductive smile.

"Yes, but to fix your arm."

"It's just a scratch."

"And I'm your sister," she said flatly.

"Fine, you win, but like I said, don't be disappointed when it turns out I was right."

Once they got to their room, Bre took his arm and cut the bullet hole wider. She could see that the bullet had just grazed him.

"I told you so."

"It still needs to be cleaned," she said, walking over to the desk and retrieving his last bottle of rum. She was about to pour it over the cut when he stopped her.

"Wait, is there anything else we can use?"

"No," she said and poured it over the cut without waiting for a response. She then took a piece of dry cloth and wrapped it around the wound, finally tying it off. "There. I'm hiding this bottle so we'll have it to keep that clean. I don't want you back in the state you were in last time."

"But we had fun," he said as he looked at her.

"Yes, but that won't stop me from hiding this bottle," she said with a smile.

"That's not nice of you." He turned to leave, and Bre followed him out.

Steven was waiting outside the door. "What are we going to do about *The West Star*? It isn't that far ahead of us."

Evans thought for a moment and then said, "Let it go. As long as they're running, they'll fear us and tell others about us."

Steven looked at him like he'd lost his mind. "You, of all people, are just going to let them get away."

"Yes. They're cowards. If they wasn't, they'd have stayed to fight. So let them spread the word about our ships."

Steven just threw his hands up and walked off, mumbling the whole time about letting them go.

Jim and Jerry looked at all the destruction they'd caused as they passed a bottle of rum back and forth.

Evans was at the helm, with Bre in his arms.

"You know, them two will be together forever," Jim said.

"No, the three of them will be together forever," Jerry quickly replied.

"What do you mean, the three of them?"

"Evans, Bre, and *The Nitingale*," Jerry said with a smile.

"What is it about this ship that makes it so special anyway?"

"Don't know, but we've all been asking that question for a while now," Hoss said as he pulled up a crate beside them.

"It's a mystery," Ray said with a laugh.

"Well, we've all heard the stories. So maybe there is some truth behind them," Rod said.

"All bullshit," Hoss said. "It's the same as Steven's and mine."

"You have to admit, it sails completely different for Evans than it does for anyone else," Steven said as he joined them.

Bre was walking out of quarter's when she looked over the ship to find Evans, when instead she saw Pike, Zack, and Brandon standing to the side. Zack was holding Pike's shirt up, and Brandon had some kind of bowl in his hand.

She waited until they were done looking each other over; then she watched as Pike went back to work.

She walked up beside of him and after thinking about it for a minute, she put her hand on his back. She made it look like she was tapping his back to get his attention. He jerked away from her hand. She looked at him with flames in her eyes, and he knew he'd been caught.

"Let me see it," was all she said.

"It's not that bad, just a bruise."

"We'll see," she said, taking him by the arm.

"Where are we going?"

"To see Evans. If he says it's just a bruise, I'll leave you alone, but if it's more than that, we're going to have a huge talk. Along with Brandon and Zack."

They reached Evans, who looked at her and then back to Pike. "What have you done now to make this woman mad?" he asked.

"Look for yourself. He said it's just a bruise, but I don't believe him."

"Why not?" Evans asked her.

"Because he smiles too much," she replied.

"Okay, let me see it," Evans said, turning to Pike.

Pike looked at them both, then took a deep breath and turned around. He lifted his shirt carefully, then pulled it up over his head.

"That is *not* a bruise," Bre said as she looked at the slash that went across his shoulders. "What happened, and why didn't you come to us with this?"

He turned around, still holding his shirt across his arms. "I was afraid that you wouldn't let me come back out."

"Where are Zack and Brandon?" Bre yelled out to the crew near her. "Find them and tell them to get to me *now*."

After a few minutes, they showed up and saw Pike holding up his shirt while Dean stitched his cut.

Bre looked at them for a moment and then said, "Look, I'll only ask this once, and if you lie to me and I find out, there will be a huge price to pay."

"Okay," they said at the same time.

"Are either of you hurt? I don't care if it's a broken fingernail. I need to know right now."

They looked at each other and then over to Evans, who told them, "Out with it!"

"I have a few bruised ribs," Brandon said. "Other than that, no. You can check if you want."

"Pull up your shirt," Evans said to him.

Once he did, they saw that his ribs were purple and turning a blackish color.

Evans pushed around on them with a hand. "None of them seem to be broken. Tell Hoss to give you some liniment to rub on it. It'll take the pain away a little. Then come right back here for a family meeting."

"Okay," Brandon said before running off.

Evans and Bre turned to Zack. "What?" he asked them. "I'm fine, nothing really." His eyes shone like diamonds.

"Pull off your shirt. Let's see," Evans told him.

Zack did as he was told, revealing a small hole in his side where it looked as though a bullet had gone through him.

"What is that?" Bre asked.

"I don't know really. I was standing over there behind Evans, and all of a sudden it felt like a bunch of bees stung me all at one time."

"The bullet," Evans said, his anger flying. "If that lowlife—"

"Enough," Bre said.

"I'd kill him again if I could," Evans said before yelling, "Darron! Bring your tools."

"We need to get the bullet out of you before it's too late," Bre said. "Remember when Evans was sick? Well, it was from a bullet."

"Fine," he said as the thought scared him.

Darron came over and looked at Zack's side. "This is going to hurt a little," he said as he picked up a pair of pliers.

"Wait," Dean said. "Here—drink, boy." He handed Zack a bottle of rum.

Zack did as he was told, and Darron poured some of the booze on his side. Then he plunged the pliers into the hole to find the bullet. After what seemed like hours, only took a few minutes for Darron pulled out the pliers along with the bullet. "Here you go. Your first bullet. Keep it for luck," he said with a smile. "Dean, it's your turn."

Dean walked over to Zack and looked at the wound for a minute. "I can't sew this up. It's too round. We'll just have to keep an eye on it. Keep it covered and clean it often. Or do I have to tell Bre to do it?"

"I'll do it," he answered.

"No, you will not. Bre or myself will," Evans said. "That's the only way we can make sure it doesn't get infected and cause you to die."

"Well, it'd be better than sitting at home," he mumbled.

Bre looked at Evans, then back to the boys. "I don't know what you're talking about. We know you was scared to show us your injuries, but it's better that you did. We wasn't going to make you stay home, not over this. Now if you had lied to me about it, then yes. All that would have done was shown us that you wasn't old enough to be out here. Owning up to your wounds proved that we was right by our assessment of you."

"She's right. As long as you're man enough to admit when you're hurt, and not keep it from us, then you're man enough to stay on," Evans said. "Now go and find work to do. You might be hurt, but not bad enough to keep you from your duties."

"That was nice of you," Hoss said after the pair had walked off. Austin stood at his side.

"Thanks. What are you doing with this one?" Evans asked, pointing to Austin.

"I've decided that because of his actions, he can stay and work for me. I can teach him some more things. Besides, he done good during all the fighting. I was so proud of him. Did I tell you he killed three men without even blinking?"

"We tried to tell you they was ready, but no. You didn't want to hear any of it," Bre said with a laugh. "Just like you don't want a girl to save your hide."

"Darling, you can save me anytime you'd like," he said as he pulled her into a bear hug.

After everything was taken care of, Bre decided to change back into her normal attire, hoping that she could stay in it a little longer than last time.

Evans followed her into the room. When she pulled off her pants and shirt, he noticed a huge bruise on her side. "What is that?"

"What?" she said, puzzled.

"That bruise. How'd you get it?"

"I don't know what you're talking about."

"This!" he said, pulling up her corset.

"I don't know," she said. "I don't even remember getting it." As she was trying to remember.

"Well, hold on. I need to rub some liniment on it." He opened the door and yelled for Brandon, asking him to bring the ointment. He then turned his attention to Bre. He took off her corset and then her undershirt to look her over. She only had the one bruise. It was in the exact shape of a fist. He knew she'd been hit hard, and he didn't understand how neither of them could recall it.

Brandon knocked on the door. "Here you are," he said once Evans had opened the door wide enough to stick his hand through.

"Thank you," he said as he shut the door.

"This stuff stinks," she said to Evans as he rubbed the liniment on her side.

"Maybe, but it helps."

"Fine," she said, then held her breath.

Once he was done, she put on one of her dresses. She looked at him and smiled. "It feels good to be a lady again."

"And what a lady you are, princess," he said, kissing her softly on the lips.

They were delayed a day as Cliff, Nunn, Jacob, and Brandon repaired the ships. They spent most of their time focusing on *The Sphinx* and *The Phoenix*. Cliff knew he could repair *The Nitingale* once they get home, so he wasn't that concerned with her at the moment.

Meanwhile, Steven, Evans, and Hoss were busy talking about letting *The Western Star* go. It was killing Steven that they weren't going after it, so he and Hoss were trying to convince Evans into pursuing it.

"Leave it alone," Evans said. "They are done gone. We have to get this load there, and I have to get them back to their ships before this whole mess puts CP Trading down for good."

"I think we need to do this," Steven said, trying to control his anger.

"No," Evans said, his flushed face betraying his anger. "This is an order. We will let them go. Besides, she's probably done changed names now. So there's no way of knowing anything."

"Fine," Steven snapped before stomping off.

"What do you want me to do about him?" Hoss asked as he and Evans watched Steven stalk off.

"Keep him out of trouble until you dock. Maybe by then he'll have calmed down," Evans said. "I'm going to have Darron make you some cannons to put on your ship, and some for Steven."

"It's about time," Hoss said with a smile.

"Well, I never thought about it before. We're on the up and up. How was I to know that we might get into trouble?"

"I know, man, I feel the same way. You never think about something like that until you need it," Hoss said. "So is it true? Are you going to finish this season out?"

"I'm thinking about it. I think it might be good for CP Trading. At least until everyone knows that you two are my men."

"What, now you think we can't take care of ourselves?" Hoss said, laughing.

Cliff walked over to them. "We're finished for the most part. I told Ray and Jake they better be finished before they reach the dock at home. If they come back unfinished, I'll skin the both of them."

"So I guess this is goodbye until the end of the season," Evans said to Hoss.

"I'll see you soon, brother. Who knows? We might run into each other again."

"Hopefully when we do it isn't in a battle."

"Or getting Steven out of trouble!" Hoss smiled.

Evans and Bre stood at the helm, his arms wrapped around her waist. They watched *The Phoenix* and *The Sphinx* sail toward America.

"Do you think them two will go after that ship?" Bre asked, wiggling around as he kissed her neck.

"No," he said, but then he paused. "This sure is a fine way of stopping a romantic moment. I'll kill them both. At least I know Hoss will stop him. He won't let Steven do anything stupid."

"What if Steven talks Hoss into going with him?"

"That will never happen," Evans said quickly. Then he looked at Bre. "Why do you do this to me?"

Just then Jim came up. "Sorry to interrupt, but I need to talk to you," he said to Evans.

"Oh, don't worry about that, Bre has done that just fine," he said, looking over to her. "What is it, Cousin?"

"I've been thinking. I want you to drop me off at Fat Louie's island. I want to lay claim to it before some other bloodthirsty pirate does. I figured it would be good for all of us. It'll give me a place of my own to berth from, and it'll give Unc another port that works for us."

"It sounds good, but what about your crew?"

"Tell them to meet me there," Jim replied.

"Who'll have your backside? There are things to think about here, Cousin."

"Don't worry. If it's okay with you, I'll take Tim and Big Jon with me. We're getting to be good friends, plus he knows the island. So it's a win-win for me."

"I don't know," Evans said. He looked around and saw Tim and Big Jon talking to Glover, so he yelled for them to come over. Once they got there, Evans looked at Glover, who could see that something was wrong.

"What is it, Cap?" Glover said hurriedly.

"Jim wants us to drop him, Tim, and Big Jon off at Fat Louie's island. He wants to take it over. I think that part's a good idea, but I don't think he should do it by himself. No offense meant to you two."

"None taken," Big Jon said with a smile. "I just think he needs someone he can trust at his side. I thought if it was okay with you, I'd go with him. I know the island and the people. So there shouldn't be much trouble."

Evans looked at him. "If you're taking care of my family, then I have no problem with it. And I think you'll do that for him. Thank you."

"I'll take over one of the open spots if you'll have me," Tim said.

"Wait," Glover said. "What about Mark?"

"He'll be fine with it," Tim said. "Besides, after sailing with all you cutthroats, I sorta miss the action."

"I know a man on the island who can take my spot," Big Jon said. "He can cook, repair sails, and do just about anything else there is to do. Plus, he's good with cannons. In fact, that's his specialty."

"I don't know," Evans said. "I only take men I know and can trust."

"You know him; his name's Donnie," Tim said.

"Damn it Donnie?" Evans asked with laughter.

"Yes, I think he goes by that sometimes."

"Okay. I'll take him if he's free," Evans said. "Cousin, I still don't like this, but I'll do it if this is really what you want."

"It is, and don't worry; I'll be fine. You'll see. But I need you to take over my loads until I get this settled."

"I can do that," he said as he looked at Bre, who gave him a loving look.

"If it makes you feel better, we can all go into town together before you leave me. That way everyone can see we mean business."

"Don't worry about that—I was planning to anyway," Evans said. "Family sticks together, no matter what."

"That's right," Bre added. "We wasn't going to drop you off and head home. I can't believe you'd think that we would!"

"Somehow I knew that, it's not in Evans to just drop him off and leave" he said before he walked away.

"Glover, you're in charge. You know where we're going, so I'm going to get some overdue shut-eye. I have a funny feeling I'll be needing it." Then he took Bre's hand and led her to their cabin.

# Chapter 9

The next day, they arrived at the island. The men lowered the sails and tied them down. Evans was dressed as if he were ready for battle. Bre was next to him, getting herself ready as well.

When they walked onto the front deck, Bre pointed at the men. "Looks like we wasn't the only ones thinking there might be trouble." As she noticed all the men was dress for battle.

"What can I say? It's my crew. They know when I need them without me ever saying a word."

"I know. It's like all of you, the ship included, are one," Bre said and kissed him. "Ready?"

"Always," he said, then looked at Glover, who was already by his side.

"We're ready, Cap. Where do we go first?"

Just then Jim walked over. "Well, I guess the first place to start is the tavern. Then we'll work our way to his office and his house and take them over as well."

"Let's get to it," Evans said, looking at his men. "Remember: Take no mercy and give none. For the rest of you who are staying on board: Keep her safe. There might be trouble, so do what you have to. We'll be back by sundown." He walked over to Pike and Zack. "Don't be afraid to fire on the town."

"We're not going with you?" Pike asked with disappointed.

"No, you two are in charge. You're the only trusted men I have for this job. Plus, I know you'll carry out my orders."

"Aye, Cap," they said simultaneously.

"That's my boys."

The rest of them were getting off the ship. After they were out of sight, a man came over to them. "I'm not taking orders from kids," he said with a laugh. "I'm in charge, and I say we go."

"We're in charge, like it or not," Zack said. "If any of the rest of you feel the same way, then you don't need to be sailing for Captain Evans."

"I'll break you in half with just one snap," the man growled to Zack.

Pike pulled out his pistol and held it on the man. "Listen here, you lonely rat. You mean nothing to us. I suggest you get back to your station before the other men have to clean your blood off the deck."

"Why, you little—" was all the man could get out before Pike shot him between the eyes. The man fell backward and landed at the feet of some of the men who had been with him.

"Like I said, we're in charge," Zack said loudly. "If you have a problem with it, then we'll settle it right now. Otherwise, I suggest you get to your stations. And as for you five rats, I think you need to get to work. Before he stinks up the whole boat."

"No, leave him," Pike said. "Let him be a reminder that we're in charge and that we won't take any drivel from any of them."

"You five come with me. I'm placing you in the holds. Evans can deal with you when he gets back," Zack said, holding his gun on them. "Let's go," he barked one last time before they began to move.

The rest of the rats went back to their stations, mumbling and whispering about the boys. They'd never seen cutthroats so young before. The rumor had to be true that they were Evans's sons. Only he could be so heartless at such a young age.

Evans and his men had split up in the town and were looking for any signs of trouble. When he and Bre walked by the courthouse, two women, followed closely by a man, came over.

"I told you it was him," one of the women said. She was dressed in her underclothes, with a robe to protect her modesty.

"Well, well. I heard you was here. It hurt our feelings that you didn't even stop by for a drink," the other woman who was a brunette, said, also dressed in underclothes and a robe.

Bre stepped between them and Evans. "If you want to keep your heads, I suggest that you turn and walk away from my husband now."

They stepped back and were silent for a minute while Evans and the man busted out laughing.

"Who's this annoying thing?" one of them asked.

"We're not women you want to mess with, honey," the other chimed in.

"I beg to differ. I'd say that *you* wouldn't want to mess with *me*," Bre said with a smile. "And to answer your question, I'm Captain Evans's wife."

"So it is true," the brunette said to him.

Evans looked at them for a minute, then at his wife. "Yes, this is my beautiful wife, Bre. So unless you don't want to lose your heads, girls, I suggest you do as she said. She means what she says."

"I'm not afraid of her," was all one got out before Bre stepped forward and punched the brunette in the nose.

"Let's go, Daisy, I think she means what she says. There's always other captains. This one's taken—by a woman as mean as him."

"Fine, you win this time, but next time you might not be so lucky as she wiped away the blood from her nose." Then the two women took off, disappearing into a house.

"Always got trouble surrounding you," the man said with a laugh.

"I should have known I'd find you hanging around here. It's good to see you, Donnie," Evans said as he clapped him on his back.

"So what brings you here?" he asked, looking over at Bre.

"As you heard, this is my wife, Bre," Evans said with a chuckle. "She'll calm down in a few. Anyway, I was looking for you. Are you sailing for anyone?"

"No, I'm taking time off."

"Is that your way of saying you're free?"

"Yes. No one wants me. They're scared of me," Donnie said. "I wouldn't know why." He barked a laugh.

"Good, come sail for me. I need a man like you."

"All right, you got yourself a deal. When do we leave?"

"When can you be ready?" Evans asked.

Donnie looked around at the ground, then behind him, then back at Evans. "I'm ready. All I have is all you see. I lost everything last night in a game."

"Damn it, Donnie, when will you learn?" Evans said, laughing. "Let's go. I have to check on Jim; then we're out of here."

"So it's true, he is taking over the island. It went like wildfire."

"It's a shame we've only been here for half a day," Evans said with a grin.

"Well, it might be because they think you're the devil himself. They're afraid of you, and by the looks of things, your wife will soon have a reputation of her own," Donnie said with a laugh.

Bre finally spoke up. "It's nice to meet you," she said to Donnie. Then she turned to Evans. "Do I have to go through this every time we make port?"

"Not all the time," he said with a sheepish smile.

She wanted to smack him, but his grin made her smile back. "Fine, you win, but just this time."

"Come on, princess," Evans said, pulling her into his arms. "I love you and only you. Those girls are in my past. You're my present and future. Don't let them bother you."

They walked on until they found Jim with the rest of his men. "Well, Cousin, it looks like we scared the island and they know you're the new king," Evans said with a laugh.

"Yep, that's all because of you," he replied. "If it wasn't for you and that damn special ship you have, none of this would've been so easy."

"I can't help if people are scared of me, or my girls," Evans said, smiling. "Maybe it's just the stories. . . . I'm not *that* bad."

Once the words left his mouth, Bre and all the men stepped away from him and looked up to the sky. Then Bre said with a smile, "Well, maybe he's right, because he didn't get hit with lightning."

"All of you are just so funny," Evans said. "Well, Cousin, you going to be all right here?"

"Yes, go on home. I'm sure Unc is worried to death that we aren't back yet. Tell my men to meet me here. I still have some business to do. Tell Unc I'll see him in a few weeks to get things set up for CP Trading.

"I will. I love you, Cousin. Take care." Evans looked at Big Jon. "Keep him safe until the rest of his men get here."

"I will, don't worry," Big Jon said as he shook his hand. "I enjoyed sailing for you. It was an honor."

"Thank you. I feel the same way. Anytime this cutthroat doesn't treat you right, you are always welcomed on my crew," Evans said, then turned to Jim. "Got to go, man. See you soon."

"That's a deal," Jim said as he hugged him goodbye. "I love you, Cousin. Bre, honey, take care of him, please."

"I'll do my best," she said before taking her turn hugging him.

Jim said farewell to the rest of his family, then went inside to get his new house set up.

On the way back to the ship, Evans and Bre ran into a young girl standing on the dock. He looked at her for a moment, then smiled at her. "I guess you're ready?" he asked.

"Yes," she said, smiling back at him. "I left word for my father to find me." She looked at Bre, who was standing beside Evans.

"Princess, this is Jeff's daughter. Olivia, this is my wife, Breanna. We call her Bre."

"Nice to meet you," she said as she reached out to take Bre's hand.

"How did you know your father was sailing for us?" Bre asked in shock.

"I didn't, but after what happened here today, I figured I was safer with Evans."

"Oh," she said with a smile. "Well, let's get you out of here."

Donnie looked over at Evans. "I believe your wife just found her a friend as evil as she is. I might need to stay here."

Evans busted out in laughter, then watched the pair of women. *Donnie might be right*, he thought to himself.

Evans and his crew went back to *The Nitingale* to get ready to sail home. Once they stepped onto the ship, Bre pulled hard on Evans's arm, pointing to the dead man lying on the deck.

"Pike! Zack!" Evans called out.

Once they arrived, he studied them for a moment. Once he realized they weren't hurt, he asked them what happened.

"They wanted to leave you here, and didn't want to listen to us, so we handled it," Pike said.

"I can see you 'handled it.' But what I want to know is, who killed him?"

"That was Pike," Zack answered. "He was saving me. I gave the order to clean it up, but Pike said to leave him."

"Why?" Evans looked at Pike.

"Because it would show the men we're in charge, and he was a reminder until you came back. I'll make them clean it up," Pike said, turning to give the order.

"No, I will. I have some more things to say to them," Evans said, anger flushing his face.

"Wait," Zack said. "I have the rest of his men in the holds. I told them they could stay there until you came back. You want me to go get them?"

"I will," Jerry said, his rage showing.

"Let's get her out to sea, where we can handle this probably," Ray said to Evans.

"Glover's already on that," Bre said as she watched Glover ordering the men to make weigh.

Once they were out to sea, Evans gathered the men together and stood in front of them. The ones who had been in the holds were up front; Jerry, Ray, and Rod held them at gunpoint. Bre, Pike, Zack, and Brandon were standing next to Evans. The rest of his trusty crew stood beside of him, facing the men.

Evans looked at them all, then at the five men who stood with guns on them. "Let me begin with this. On my ship, I give the orders. If I place someone in charge, I mean for them to hold fast to my word. I do not allow anyone on this ship to undermine my authority. I have a very low tolerance for mutiny, the punishment for which is *death*. It's the code you all signed when you joined my crew. So if anyone has a problem with my choices, speak now. Because after today, if any of you sail for me again, I expect you to follow my orders."

The men remained silent for some time, until one old man spoke up. "Cap, we love you. We've gone with you for as long as we can remember. We would never do anything to hurt you or your family. Those that done this aren't part of us. They were new men; this was their first time out with you. I . . . we think your boys done a mighty fine job. They'll make nice caps of their own one day. They have what it takes."

"Thank you, Sniffy," Evans said to him. "I appreciate all of you. So now that we have that settled, we can deal with these rats. Men, any last words?"

The five men looked at each other and then back at Evans. One stepped up. "Captain, I know that we really don't know each other, but I had no choice in this. That man your son killed was my brother. He made me go with him. I have a family at home that I'm trying to take care of. If you leave me alive, I promise I'll never do any of this again."

"Coward!" one of the other men yelled. "Just die and don't disrespect your family—and your four little children."

"I'll make sure they get your wages," Evans said as he looked at the man pleading for his life. Then he gave the order to fire.

"Wait!" the man yelled out.

Evans looked at him. "What now?"

"You're still going to kill me?"

"Yes."

"Then you *are* the devil."

"In that case, I'll see you in hell," Evans said. "Fire, and this time don't stop for nothing."

In a moment, all five men had been killed with clean shots.

Sniffy came up to Evans. "You did good. I mean, not believing that lowlife. He ain't nothing but trouble—has been all his life."

Evans furrowed his brow and looked at him. "So you knew him?"

"Knew *of* him. One of the men was telling me about him. All he was doing was trying to make you feel sorry for him. I think you did a mighty fine job."

"Thank you, old man."

"One more thing, Cap. That wife of yours—she's something. I've never seen anything like her. Any woman would've run, but she stood tall at your side. She also has a decent stance with a sword. You done mighty good with that one. She was made just for you."

"Thank you," he said with a smile. "She's everything to me, and more."

"Anytime, Cap," he said before walking away.

Evans went to his wife and looked at her. "I know you must be tired. Go rest some. We'll be home in a day. I'm sure our son is missing his mother."

"And his father," she said with a sleepy smile. "I think I will." She kissed him goodnight and went to their room.

Nunn joined Evans and Glover, who were standing at the helm. "Cap, I hope you don't mind, but while we was helping Jim, I picked up my little brother, Jamie. He hasn't ever sailed before, but he's a fast learner.... he pauses and signs, then reaches up and takes off his hat. I couldn't leave him behind."

"That's fine," Evans said. "We'll find a place for him." He looked at the young boy. He resembled his brother, but skinny, to skinny for Evans opinion. He could tell by looking at this little boy he pegged for being around nine maybe ten years old. That he had a rough life. "Nice to have you aboard."

"Thank you," he said. "I'll try hard to not let you down—or my brother."

"Thank you, Cap," Nunn said before going back to work.

On the way back to their post, Jamie looked at his brother. "Are you sure you want to sail for him? He just killed five men. Is it safe?"

"Yes. That was because they mutinied. The punishment for that is death. It's just the way it has to be to keep order."

"I see . . . but why kill them?"

"It's like this: If you don't stop them from mutinying, then who do you trust with a sword at your back? Because if they could mutiny without consequence, they'd be doing it all the time. Who's to say—*you* might be the target of their mutiny."

"Oh," was all he said. Then they went back to work.

# Chapter 10

Everything went well on their way home. Bre woke up to find Evans missing from bed. So she arose and cleaned herself up. Then she made her way to the helm.

"Morning, princess, did you sleep well?"

"Yes, and I know you checked on me."

"How do you know that?" he asked with a smile.

"Because the bottle of rum on the desk is empty."

"That damn rum," Evans said. "I had to know that you was all right."

"I love you," Bre said with a happy sigh, reaching to kiss him. "Have you been here all night?"

"What can I say? It's my time. Besides, it was clear and the moon was out full. I hate that you missed it."

"Me too," she said as she looked out and saw Hell coming up in the distance. She turned to Evans. "Are we going straight home or to the big island first?"

"We're going home. I figured Ray and Jerry can make sure the men get home. Besides, we have nothing of value on the ship, so there's nothing to off-load."

Just then Pike, Zack, and Brandon walked up, looking down and out.

"What's wrong with you three?" Bre asked. They had changed back into their normal attire, but they still didn't look the same as they had when they left the island over two months ago.

"Do we have to tell Mom and Dad everything?" Brandon asked her.

"I think the less they know, the better," Bre said.

"Whose mom and dad will be there?" Olivia asked Bre.

"My parents. We don't need to tell them everything."

"I thought these boys was Evans's kids. Look at them—they're just as ruthless and tough as he is."

"No," Bre said, smiling. "They're his brothers-in-law. He only wished they was his, but in some way I think they are."

Dean walked over to take the helm. "Like them dressed like that will work. Look at them, they're men now. They'll see the change in them, and in you. In my culture, it is a honor to become a man."

Zack was fooling with his shirt collar. "I hate this. It's too tight and hot."

Bre looked at the island, then back to her brothers. She knew she'd pay for this, but she had to. "Go and change. Be who you was born to be. I'll deal with them."

They all looked at her, then grinned and ran off to change back into the clothes that suited them.

Glover ordered the cannon to be fired at that moment, to let everyone know they were pulling into port.

Everyone was waiting on the dock as they pulled in. The boys were back, dressed as themselves. Bre was the first one off. She ran to her mother, who held her baby. With haste, Bre took her son from her mother and pulled him into a tight hug, kissing him all over.

Bre was interrupted when she heard her mother say, "Oh my, how will I explain this to the women in Charles Towne?"

"What?" Bre asked, turning to see the boys getting off the ship. "If this doesn't show you that they belong here, nothing will."

Wendy walked over to Evans as he got off the ship. "Here, I thought you might need this," she said with a smile, handing him a bottle of rum. Then she rushed to Cliff to welcome him home.

Evans was heading toward his family when a man stopped him. "I'm so glad you're back. That father-in-law of yours has worked us to death. He had us building rooms, clearing paths, repairing the shacks, and working in the forge."

Glover looked over. "Oh shit," he said. "What in the world was he doing in there?"

Evans looked at them, then back to the bottle Wendy had given him. "What are you going on about?" he asked, returning his attention to the man. "What room, and what was he building in the forge?"

"The new room in your house. He calls it a library for the kids. It's full of all kinds of books, maps, and desks. It was a nightmare. Everything had to be perfect. Then he decided that the forge was too small, so he had us make it larger. It took us a week just to move everything around the way he thought it should be."

"He didn't!" Glover said, then took the rum from Evans. "I think I need this."

Evans just smiled and took his bottle back. "It can't be that bad. Just take your wife home and we'll deal with it in the morning."

Glover shook his head and walked over to claim his wife, mumbling the whole way.

"What about my cave?" Evans asked the man.

"It was the only place we could keep from him—it's safe. I can't say that about other parts of the island. Wendy was ready to kill him. He went and made corrections on her rum shack, but I have to say it did turn out nice. He knows what he's doing, but he's killing us in the process just the same. Can we go back to doing nothing? We like it better like that."

"Yes, go and relax," Evans said with a smile.

Bre and her parents went to the house, the boys trailing behind them. Evans knew this would be hard for them, but he also knew it would be better if he let them handle it alone.

They passed Evans's father, who stopped them. "Ah shit," he said as he looked at them. "All of you have blood on your hands." Then he glanced at Bre. "I told you to stay your ass at home. Now look at you. You'll never be the same again."

"What are you talking about?" she said, looking down at her hands and at her brothers.

"Killing, you all have killed. It's all over you. You *stink* from it." Then he yelled out as loudly as he could, "Evans, get up here now!"

Dean and Donnie watched Evans head to his father. Dean looked over at Donnie. "It's a shame, a man that isn't afraid of nothing—fought hurricanes and battles—is running like a scared pup."

"If that was my father, I'd run too. That man is as ruthless as his son. This'll be good," Donnie said with a smile.

"Well, I think I'm going to walk around and get used to the island. I was never one to watch as a man gets the third degree from his father," Dean said before making himself scarce.

"Wait up!" Donnie called. "Might as well go with you. That way there's no witness to this."

Evans reached his father, who looked at him and asked, "Why?"

Ray, Jerry, and Rod were right behind Evans. "It wasn't that bad—we was never in no danger," Ray said.

"Really," he said and took Zack's sword from him. "This was new when you left. Looks like it's been in battle."

"Unc, we only did what we had to," Jerry said.

"That's another thing. You had all the captains out there fighting. What if something had happened? Where would that leave the company, son?"

"We'll talk about this later, Dad," Evans said before he, Jerry, Ray, and Rod walked off for the cave.

Darrell turned to Bre. "I have to be hard on him, but I'm glad they were all together." He paused before asking, "Where's Jim?"

"We dropped him off. Evans can tell you more about that, but he's okay."

"Well, I see they did take care of you."

"Yes, but you was right about all of it," she said, holding her baby tighter. "I'm glad they were there, but they are a bunch of cutthroats from hell."

"That's my boys," he said with a proud smile.

"I heard stories about you and their fathers, about when you all sailed together," Bre said.

"I'll kill him," was all he said before walking off to find his son.

They went on to the house. Once they walked in, Bre's little sister ran to her and hugged her. "I missed you!" she said with a huge smile. "I have so much to tell you."

"It'll have to wait. We're having a family meeting right now," her father said. "Everyone in the library."

Once inside the new library, Bre just stared at it. "Where did all of these books come from?"

"Some I found lying around, others I brought in from Charles Towne, but we'll talk about that later."

"What's all this about?" Bre asked her dad.

"This is about your brothers," he answered, studying the boys. "If I didn't know better, I'd swear they were all Evans."

Bre looked at them and then back at her father. "Okay, well let's get this over with."

"We're leaving in a few days. When we go, we're taking Kandice, Bobby, and a few others with us. I'm leaving Pike, Brandon, and Zack here in your care—on one condition."

"Anything," Zack said.

"They have to attend school; they have to be educated. I know they'll sail, but during time off, I want them in school. If I find out they're not, then I will come back and take them home, and I'll blame you for their failure."

"I will, Daddy, I promise I will," Bre said eagerly.

"Good. I had the men build a schoolhouse next to the church. I figured the other kids on the island would need it. So all you have to do is find a suitable teacher. There are schoolbooks already there for all ages."

"Okay, I'll find one in the morning."

"Another thing. I want you to know that I entered a partnership with Darrell. My boys will be running my share of the business one day, so I want Evans to teach them all he can about it."

Bre looked at him like he had lost his mind, but she didn't say anything.

"Your sister's found a new beau. I'm putting him to work in Charles Towne." He paused and took a deep breath. "So now that all this is settled, tell me: How bad was it?"

"It really wasn't that bad," Pike said quickly. "We just had to do what was needed. No one was hurt, so everything was good. It was mainly cannon fire."

"Well, that wasn't that bad then," he said, then turned to Bre. "I'll let you spend time with your baby. He's crawling now! And I'm sure Evans has work for the boys."

The next morning, Evans watched his wife as she sat out on the balcony, playing with the baby.

"Morning," she said with a smile. "What's my captain going to do today?"

"I'm going to get things done around here. I already sent Jim's ship to him. Jerry and Ray left last night. So it's just us until I have to go."

"Sounds nice," she said as she watched him reach down to play with the baby. "So what did you think about the new library?"

"I can't believe he done that. It's nice, but really?"

"Shh! He might hear you." She paused. "I have some good news for you."

"Really? What might that be?"

"The boys are staying with us. Under one condition. We'll have to make sure they get an education. So I have to find them a teacher."

"Not until hurricane season," he said with a smile as he stood up. "They'll be with me, and they can't do both at the same time. I need you to go to the big island and find a friend of mine. Her name is Renee Moore."

"For what?" Bre asked.

"Tell her I need for her to find Tullis. I need some more cottages built for the new men. Also, can you check on the girls and get them settled in town, until their houses are built?"

"Okay. I need to get some things from there anyway."

"I should check on the ship. Then I need Dean to fix up my weapons." He stopped and looked at his wife, a smile on his face. "I love you, princess. Make sure you find me before you leave." He reached down and kissed her.

"I will honey," she said.

Evans went downstairs and found the boys eating breakfast. "Let's go. We have work to do."

They didn't say a word—just grabbed whatever they could and followed him out. They went to the ship first, where Cliff and Nunn's little brother were already at work.

"How long will she be before we're ready?" Evans asked Cliff.

"She isn't that bad. I could have her ready in a day or so. I'm just doing some improvements on her."

"We have a week before our load's ready, so that will give you more time," Evans said, climbing on board.

"Cap, I sure could use the boys today, if that's all right with you," Cliff said.

"That's fine. Just make sure they work and don't sit around and get lazy."

"You know I will," Cliff said before looking at the boys and beginning to dish out orders.

Evans went on to collect his weapons and ran into Donnie and Nunn.

"Come with me and I'll show you around," Evans said, weapons in hand.

They never said a word; they just followed him. They reached the forge, where Dean and Glover were already at work.

"I see he didn't mess things up too bad," Evans said with a laugh.

"Actually, he didn't do so bad! I forgot we had most of this stuff. Here, look," he said as he pointed at four cannons that were neatly stacked. "Look over there," he said, gesturing to the wall. "Look at the guns and parts—or over there, at the swords and knifes. How could I forget about all this?" Glover asked, as if in shock.

"Well, we can put them on *The Nitingale* in case we run into Steven or Hoss. Here," Evans said, setting down his weapons. "I need you to repair these."

"I have my hands full, fixing all the weapons, and I only have two hands. Dean is good, but he isn't that fast yet. So it'll take a while." He paused, then looked up at Evans. "Where's the boys? I sure could use them."

"Cliff done beat you to them."

"Not a problem," Donnie said. "I know how, and I bet I can out-work you."

"Donnie, no," Evans said in a warning tone.

"Fine, just trying to have some fun." He laughed out load.

"You know, with a few improvements on these axes, they'd work much better," Dean said.

"What do you mean?" Glover asked.

"Look," he said, holding out his own weapon. "See my tomahawk? If your axes was just a little more narrower and had just a little less weight to them. . . ."

Glover looked at it, nodding. "I get what you're saying."

They walked off together, talking about making the changes, as Bre's father came over. "Hello, son, can we talk?"

"Sure. You want to walk?" Evans asked as they took off toward the back side of the island.

A little while later, Bre approached Glover and looked at the other three men in the forge. "Glover, can you fix my sword and my rifle, pretty please?"

"Yes, what's wrong with the rifle?"

"I messed up the sights, and it has a couple of dents from when I hit a man with it."

"Okay, princess, I'll get started on them right now and will have them done in a while."

"I see that Evans was here, as she spotted his weapons on the table. Where did he go? I know he isn't on the dock."

"He took off with your father," Nunn said, looking up.

"Aye, Evans took him to the back side. I think he was trying to keep him away from the cave," Dean said with a laugh.

"All right, well I'm heading to the big island now. If you see Evans, tell him that I was looking for him, but couldn't find him, and that I'm taking Linds and Olivia with me." Then she was gone.

Nunn looked at Glover. "Tell me, why are you jumping on her weapons, but told Evans his had to wait?"

"It's Bre," Glover said as he held up her rifle, looking at it. "That girl is special, but she sure can mess up a gun. Look at that dent in the barrel."

"What's so special about her?" Nunn asked, examining the dent.

"For a rich girl from Charles Towne, she's come a long way." He started taking the gun apart.

"What was the talk about her being kidnapped? You said that was a different story for another day," Nunn said. "It's another day now."

"Yeah, I did," Glover said. "If you really want to know, I'll tell you—after you get us a bottle of rum."

Nunn returned quickly with four bottles of rum and handed each man his own bottle. "Okay, ready," he said as he pulled up a box.

Dean looked Glover. "Make it good," he said as he laughed.

Glover took a swig of rum, cleared his throat, and began, "It was about two years ago. We were all sitting in a tavern we frequented a lot back in the day. We were spying on Robert and found out that he wanted Price to kidnap his daughter. As fate would have it, we intervened, killing Price and taking Bre. We sent word that we had her . . . her three little brothers—Brandon, Pike, and Zack—tagged along. They was trying to save her, but Brandon broke his leg. We made our way to Augustine.

"While we was all in town one day, Bre was attacked by one of the men on the boat. Evans was getting her set up in an inn; he was going to leave her and her brothers there. When we came back to the boat, we saw what had happened. Hoss set weigh as Evans made sure Bre wasn't hurt—the man who'd attacked her was killed, of course. Bre fell in love with Evans that day for sure, and we all knew he done fell for her when he laid eyes on her.

"Damn, that girl was a handful. Pushed Evans to the end and back several times. If it'd been anyone else, he would've killed them. She faked being sick to get his attention; she rode out a tempest tied to him at the helm."

"You have to be kidding us," Donnie said.

"No," they heard a man say behind them. It was Cliff. "Sorry for interrupting, but I sent the boys here, and when they didn't return, I thought I'd better find them."

Glover turned then and noticed that the three boys had joined the circle and were listening to the story.

"That's why I installed a larger helm—so when that crazy girl decides to tie herself to him again, there'll be more room," Cliff said in a laugh.

"That's when we knew they was meant for each other. They fought and cared for each other while we where in the Florida Straights when we stopped for repairs—mostly fought. A woman came up to Evans, and Bre ran her off by saying they was married."

"I could see that," Donnie said. "I watched her run two off just a few days ago."

"We got back here, and she took up with everyone fast, started to learn how to fight. She also kept after Evans to admit his feelings for her. Then when he found out she wasn't Robert's daughter but was his niece instead, everything changed. Evans got hurt, and Bre nursed him back to the land of the living. He finally asked her to be his wife, but before they got married, he went after Robert, and guess who snuck onboard?"

"I did," Brandon said, looking at the pile of swords in the corner.

"That's right. Bre was caught by Robert, and Hoss gave her the order to get away from him. She did well, if I do say so myself. She stabbed him in the leg and got free. Then we heard the shot. She'd killed him with the bullet Robert himself had put into Evans's leg."

"Now that you all know the story, let's get back to work," Cliff said. "Daylight's wasting." He grabbed Glover's bottle of rum and walked off. "Hurry up, boys!" he yelled before disappearing from sight.

"What are you looking at, boy?" Glover asked Zack.

"This sword, I like it. What is it?"

"It's a Bagua—a Chinese sword."

"It has enormous cutting and slashing power. More so than a normal sword. It helps promote strength and agility," Donnie said.

"I want one," Zack said quickly before turning to Glover. "Can you make me one?"

"I tell you what—you can have this one. I think you've earned it. Pike, you and Brandon pick one out as well."

Pike smiling from ear to ear, looked at them and found a sword that was similar to Zack's, but smaller. "What's this one? I like it." He picked it up.

"That's a Willow Leaf. It's known as the classic Chinese sword. The tapered blade is to aid in balance, and it's perfectly shaped for cutting, slashing, and chopping strokes," Donnie explained.

"Can I have this one?" Pike asked Glover, who was busy looking at Donnie.

"Yes," he said without looking to see which sword Pike had chosen. "How do you know so much?" he asked Donnie.

"I've been around," he said with a smile.

"I'm not sure about the swords. I'd like to learn how to fight with the tomahawks like you do," Brandon said to Dean.

"I'll teach you. Here, you can start with these," he said, handing him two from the shelf.

# *Chapter* 11

**B**re had reached the big island. Olivia had gone with her to keep her company. They went to a small building where Evans had said she could find Renee. Bre looked at the building for a minute, then went inside. She walked over to a woman who was seated at a long table with a small pile of papers in front of her.

"Excuse me," Bre said in a low voice. "I'm looking for Renee."

"You found her," the woman said as she stood up. She was taller then Bre, well dressed, and had her hair pulled back into a bun. She looked very elegant for a woman in her late twenties. "What can I do for you today?"

"Evans sent me to acquire your services."

"Well, you must be Breanna. I was wondering when we'd meet. What does he need this time?"

"He needs temporary housing for some young ladies, whose husbands sail for us. He said you could find them a nice place away from harm."

"Lucky for him, we had a house open up next to his parents. You can't get no safer than that," she said with a smile.

"Sounds good. What do you need?" Bre asked.

"Not a thing, just tell him he can settle up once it's done. Is there anything else I can do for you?" she asked, digging through a drawer.

"Can you tell me where I can find a man named Tullis?" Bre asked.

"Yes, he's working—always working. I think today you'll find him at 504 West Street. Here's the key for the house. I'm sure you know where to find it."

"Thank you," Bre said. "I'll tell Evans you're waiting for him to settle up."

Next, Bre went to the store. She knew that Evans would kill her if he found out she was wandering the streets just the three of them without one of his trusted men at their side. She began to enter the storefront but found her father-in-law standing outside.

"Can you help me for a minute?" she asked, walking up behind him.

"First things first: never walk up behind someone like me. Second, what do you need?"

"Evans needs Tullis. Renee told me he's working at 504 West Street. Can you send someone to get him for me? We both know how Evans is about me being out without on of his men at my side," Bre said with a smile.

"Yes, I'll send someone. Where are you heading off to?"

"To get the girls from the inn, and then back here to get their accounts set up. Then I'll take them to their new home."

"Be careful, there's a lot of strange folks coming in today from the docks. I don't like the looks of some of them. On second thought. . . ." He yelled out for Kinkaid.

"What is it now?" Kinkaid asked, walking over.

"I want you to escort my daughter-in-law around town. Keep her safe, and don't let her out of your sight for a second."

"Yes, I know you or Evans will gut me like a fish," he said with a dry laugh.

"You're set, my dear. I'll have Adam go after Tullis. They should be here when you get back."

"Thank you," she said, giving him a hug.

She and Kinkaid went toward the inn; inside, she found Brittany sitting at a table by herself.

"Where are the others?" Bre asked as she walked closer to the table.

"They're upstairs," she said in a low voice. "Is David okay?"

"Yes, he's fine. He's sailing with Evans. I'm here to get you all set up. I found you a house to stay in until yours is finished on the island, and we'll get you an account set up at the store."

"Okay," she said. "I'll get the others. It shouldn't take long."

"I need to settle up with the innkeeper. I'll be waiting outside for you." Bre approached the innkeeper's desk and, with a polite smile, asked, "How much do they owe you?"

"What's the name?"

"It's either under CP Trading or under Evans's name; I'm not sure."

"You owe me . . . nothing. This account has already been taken care of," he said before hurrying into the back room.

Kinkaid laughed. "You know you're married to the devil, right.?"

Bre turned to him. "How long have you known my husband?"

"Since he was a lad. I used to sail with Captain Darrell until he retired. Now I just stick around to see what kind of trouble they find."

"Oh," she said as she studied his face.

The girls came down the stairs, each holding a bag, and one was also carrying a baby. Bre looked at them; the way they were dressed wouldn't do for this island. Since she only knew Brittany, she introduced herself to the rest of the women.

"Nice to meet you," the woman with the baby said after shaking Bre's hand. "I'm Ashley, Ray's wife. Is he okay?"

"Yes. He's sailing for us on *The Phoenix* under Steven's command," she replied, smiling at the little boy in Ashley's arms. He was just about as big as his mother. "How old is he?"

"Two," she said with a smile.

"I have son who's almost a year old. They'll be good friends one day."

"I'm Chrissie," the other girl said. "My husband is Jacob, but we all call him Jake. I take it he's okay?"

"Yes, he's fine. He's on *The Sphinx* under Hoss."

"It's a good thing you split them up," a girl coming down the steps said. "Them together, and you'd have your hands full," she said with a laugh. "I'm Brittany's sister, Jasmine."

"Nice to meet you," Bre said, smiling. "Well, if you ladies will come with me, we can get you taken care of."

They went up the street to the CP General Store. "I'll set you all up with an account here. Brittany, I'll put Jasmine on yours for now. But first let's go to the dress shop. We need to get you some dresses."

The seven women, along with Kinkaid, walked inside the shop.

"This is nice!" Ashley said.

"Look at these dresses. We can never afford anything like this," Jasmine whispered.

Bre looked over at the counter girl. "Where's Evans's mother?"

"In the back; I'll get her," the girl said, disappearing behind a curtain. A few minutes later, Evans's mother walked out and embraced her daughter-in-law, then looked at the four girls standing there.

"These are the new girls. Their husbands now work for CP Trading Company."

"Then they need to look the part," she said. "Let's get you into some proper dresses! Our men's wives dress like ladies. If I'd known about this sooner, I would've already had you dressed like proper ladies. Bre, honey, get with Katie to set up their accounts." Then she took the girls into the back room.

Bre and Katie discussed details of the account, and then waited for the women to emerge from the back of the shop. Some time later, they all came out, looking completely different. They looked more like women than barmaids. All five of them had beautiful, long dresses on that hugged in the right spots, and covered in all the right places. They was dressed like true ladies, and it did them all justice, and she could tell they felt better being dressed in proper clothing and not in rags.

"You done well," Bre said, beaming. "Now we have to go next door and get them set up over there. Love you," she said to her mother-in-law.

"Girls, you can learn a lot from this one, if you stay with her. She's the perfect example of a true lady," Delania said them all as the pride and love beemed from her voice.

Bre saw her father-in-law standing there. He just looked at Bre with knowing eyes. In return, she simply smiled at him.

They went inside the general store and Darrell said, "Randy and Liza get them set up. Bre, this is Tullis."

"Nice to meet you," she said to him.

"The pleasure is mine. So what is it I can do for you, ma'am?"

"Well, Evans wants you to come back with me. He needs you to build some homes for us. He said you'd understand how important this is and that you would be paid well for your time. He'll have a full crew waiting for you."

"I'll be ready in a few minutes then," he said as he turned to get his tools.

"When the girls are ready, we'll show them to their new accommodations," Bre said to Darrell. "By then Tullis should be back so I can head home."

"Sounds good," he said. "I'll go and see what's taking so long."
He went inside to check on things.

"Well, well. I told you the next time we ran into each other you
wouldn't be so lucky," a voice said behind Bre.

She turned around with her hand on her pistol. There were the
two whores she'd had to deal with earlier, and they had a man with
them. She only had one shot. She could handle the two of them, but
not them and the man.

"What brings you to my island?" Bre asked smugly.

"Is this the woman you was talking about?" the man asked.

"Yes, this is her," Daisy said.

"Let's take a look. She doesn't look so tough without Evans
around. I need some love anyway," he said, stepping closer to Bre.

"Walk away," Bre warned, but he continued moving closer to her.

"Come here, this won't hurt much," he said.

Thoughts of the last time she'd heard those words came flying
back to her. She looked at him and smiled. "You're right," she said as
she pulled out her pistol.

"Oh, you want to play like that?" he asked, not retreating.

Bre just pulled the trigger and watched as the man fell to his
knees. She then turned to the women. Daisy's friend was holding her
hands over her face; Daisy simply smiled at her and said, "You only
had one shot, my dear. Looks like you're in trouble now."

Bre returned her smile as she turned the pistol in her hand, holding the barrel like a battle-ax. By the time everyone walked outside
to see what was going on, Bre was fighting Daisy, who was pinned
between a barrel and a corner. Meanwhile, Daisy's friend screamed,
"Help! She's killing her!" while tearing at Bre's backside.

Bre struck with everything she had. Every time Daisy had a
chance to move, Bre would pin her down again. Finally the other
woman grabbed Bre by her hair and pulled her up, giving Daisy a
chance to move.

Bre turned around and hit Daisy's friend with one swift swing, catching her in the mouth with the butt of the pistol.

"That isn't going to happen," Olivia said when she noticed Daisy coming up behind Bre with a piece of wood.

Bre turned and saw that Daisy's friend was staggering while trying to move in closer. Bre just smiled and said, "So you want some more?" She aimed and threw a punch; she could feel something pop under her fist as she hit the woman's nose. Turning around, Bre saw that Olivia had Daisy on the ground and was hitting her with a chunk of wood—which Bre immediately took away from her.

Finally Darrell yelled, "That's enough! Adam, take these girls to the docks and put them on the first ship out of here. Bre, you and Olivia come with me so I can get you cleaned up."

"One minute," Bre said to him. Then she turned to the woman. "If you ever cross my path again, I will kill you both."

Daisy glared at her. "Just because you're dressed like a lady doesn't make you better than us. You're a whore just like we are."

"Adam, get them out of her now, or Bre will kill them," Darrell ordered.

"I am a lady," Bre said to the two women, "and I have all the proof I need to know that, as well as anyone."

"Really, and what might that be?" Daisy asked.

"I'm Evans's wife," Bre answered, smiling. "Like I said, if I see you again, I'll kill you where you stand."

Brittany turned to Bre's mother-in-law. "I thought you said she was a proper lady."

"She is, just with some backbone," she replied as Bre walked by them.

# Chapter 12

It took a moment for Bre to realized that everyone was standing around, watching her. She looked at her torn, bloody dress. Her hair was a mess, and she knew she'd soon have a black eye.

Darrell looked at his wife. "Reminds me of when we first got married," he said with a smile. "Get her cleaned up so I can take her home," he told Katie.

Darrell announced that he would take the girls to their new house. Olivia said she wanted to stay with Bre, who looked at her and asked, "Why?"

"The safest place is by your side. Plus, I figure between the two of us, we can handle whatever. Everyone needs someone to cover their backside."

"Oh hell," was all he said as he turned to lead the girls home. He knew that Evans was in trouble now for sure. He knew Bre, wasn't going to let this go away soon. "I'll be back in a little while," he told his wife with a kiss.

Tullis walked up after everything had calmed down. "Where is everyone" he asked Adam.

"Boss took the new girls to their house, and Bre's next door getting changed," he said.

"So it's true. I heard she whipped two girls and shot a man," Tullis said.

"It was like nothing I've seen before—not from a lady," Adam said.

"Aye, she sure is the perfect match for Evans. Both of them have the same attitude, and temper," Kinkaid added.

Just then Richard cleared his throat, making his presence known. They all turned to him. Adam stared at him for a moment before asking, "What are you doing here?"

"I'm looking for Bre. Is she still here?" he asked, placing a wooden box on the counter.

"Why? You going to arrest her?" Adam asked.

"No. What she did was self defense in my book. I have something for her."

"Well, that'll ease everyone's mind," Kinkaid said as he headed back to work.

"In that case, I'll let her know you're here," Adam said before walking off.

"I heard you're going to work for Evans for awhile. When are you going?" Richard asked Tullis.

"When Bre's ready," he replied, acknowledging the trouble in Richard's eyes.

"I need you to give him a message for me. Tell him that the man Bre killed. . . . His brother's here, camping out down at the tavern. He'll be looking for her, to set things right. He doesn't know that Bre is Evans's wife, so he might—hell, we both know what he'll do. Just tell him," Richard said as he went toward the back room.

"It's nice to see you," Bre said with a smile when she saw Richard. "What can I do for you?"

"I wanted to give you this. When I saw them, you popped into my mind. Then, after today's events, I knew they were made for you."

"What?" She looked at him, not sure of what he was talking about. "I thought you was here to arrest me."

"Never. You did what anyone would do in your place. You was just defending yourself." He laid a box down on her lap.

She looked at the wooden box, which was the prettiest she'd ever seen. It was made from cedar and when she opened it, the smell filled the room. She moved a piece of red silk out of the way and let out a gasp when she saw the two pistols lying there.

"They're one of a kind. They were made for a king, but either he never got them or he decided he didn't want them. Whatever the cause, they're yours now."

"I can't," she said, her eyes wide as she looked at the guns.

"Yes, you can," he said. "I have to go."

Before he could leave the room, Bre got up and hugged him. "Thank you." She gazed at the pistol in her hand. "It's something."

"Like I said, I thought of you." Then he was gone.

Bre studied the guns. They were just alike, with ivory handles that featured carvings of roses as well as gold and silver inlays. They were magnificent.

They returned to the island, and Bre and Olivia got off the small boat. Bre noticed that the only one on the dock was Cliff.

"Bre, I want you to get to the house," her father-in-law said.

"I will, but I need to drop my pistol off to Glover first," she said. "Then I'll go home. Stop worrying so much. We're home now."

"Easier said than done," he muttered. "Where's Evans?" he asked Cliff.

"He and all the other lazy bums are at the forge," Cliff said.

"Damn it, let's go." He broke into a run toward the forge.

Cliff looked at Tullis. "What gives?"

"Bre got into some trouble in town, and there will be more."

"Bloodshed?"

"Probably," Tullis said.

"It's about time. I'm bored to death. Let's go, I don't want to miss this!"

Bre reached the forge before the rest of them. She immediately walked over to Glover. "I need you to fix this for me," she said, handing him her gun.

"Didn't you leave here in a yellow dress?" Evans asked, studying her.

"Yes, she did," her father said, "and your hair was up in one of them twist thingies you do."

Just then Evans looked up and saw his father standing there with that look of anger and with trouble brewing, that all of them knew all too well.

"What the hell happened?" Evans said as he jumped up.

"Whatever it was, she took it out on her pistol," Glover said.

Bre didn't say anything. Instead, she put the cedar box down in front of Glover. "I also need you to check these guns out."

"Back to what happened in town," Evans said, making his way to her.

When he got closer, his father stepped between them. "Son, I think it's best if we handle this after she gets to the house."

"No, I want to know right now what's going on. My wife comes home dressed differently, her gun in pieces." Then he noticed her trying to hide her eye with her hair. He stepped forward and moved the strand of hair out of the way to reveal her black eye. His eyes flashed red. When he again asked her what had happened, he gritted his teeth so hard she was afraid he'd break them.

Bre looked at him, then smiled. "I love you."

"Bre," her father said. "Stop playing around and tell us what happened to you."

She looked around at all the men standing around her. They were all standing on edge, waiting to find out what had happened. She could see the fire in their eyes. "Okay," she said as she took a deep breath. She'd rather fight a group of men or take her chances with those girls again than tell her husband and his ruthless crew what had occurred. "While I was in town, that stupid woman from that island—well, she and her friend were there. They had a man with them. He . . . well. . . ."

"He tried to take Bre's virtue," her father-in-law said for her. "But she shot him before he could succeed, and then turned the gun up and fought the two women off. We had to break it up before them two," he pointed at Bre and Olivia, "killed them girls."

"What did you do with the girls?" Evans asked, trying to get things straight in his head.

"I had Adam put them on the first ship out of here. It was heading to Charles Towne."

"All hell!" Pike, Zack, Brandon, Bre's father, and Evans said simultaneously.

Bre just smiled. "I'm going to check on my baby. I'll see you later, after you calm down and come home," she said as she reached to kiss him.

Glover stopped her by asking, "Where'd you get these guns?"

"Richard gave them to me. He said something about them being one of a kind, something about made for a king. I was really to mad to listen to it all, so next time I see him I will ask him the story again. I think they might be worth something," she said before walking away.

"You think?" he said, turning the box around so Evans could get a look. "Ivory handles with gold and silver inlays. These guns have more flash than yours and mine put together."

Tullis looked at Evans. "Now that she's gone, I have a message from Richard. He said that the man she killed, well his brother's in town. He's captain of *The Rosslea*. He plans to get her the next time she's in town. He doesn't know she's your wife. All he knows is he wants blood for his brother."

"Cliff, go to Wendy and tell her that Bre needs some of her salve. Tell her to get Bre drunk or give her some tea or something. Just keep her busy. Then hurry back. We're going to fight."

"It's about time," Cliff said.

"Men, get all the weapons you can carry. Bob, will you show Tullis where we need the new houses built?"

"Not this time. I'm going with you," Bob said as he looked through the weapons.

"Bob, stay. If something happens to him, she'll need you," Darrell said.

"Okay," he said, looking at Evans. "Be careful and come home just as fast as you left 'cause once she finds out we've all had it. . . . Come on, Tullis," he said, leaving before he could change his mind

The men left on *The Nitingale* and sailed for the big island. Once they docked, they easily found *The Rosslea*, but it was empty.

Glover looked at Evans. "You know we can't use our weapons in the tavern. What's the plan of action?"

"To kill them all!" Zack and Pike said at the same time.

"I like the way you two think," Dean said.

"They don't know who she is, so we have that in our favor," Cliff added. "If we just go and have a drink—or a few—then we can find them and follow them out to kill them."

Evans agreed, knowing the whole time it was a lie. Because when he saw them, he was going to kill them all. The glow in his eyes said it. Glover just shook his head as he went to gather more weapons.

They made their way to the tavern. Once inside, they looked around.

Adam and Kinkaid were sitting at the bar. They took one look at Evans and smiled. "We told you he'd show," they both said to the man behind the bar.

Spires looked at Evans and his men. This place wouldn't look the same after they were finished. He knew that talking to Evans was hopeless, so he just turned his head and went back to work, while there was still work to do.

Adam walked over to Evans. "Your wife was something else today."

"Not now," Cliff told him, shoving Adam away from them.

Evans gave Cliff a look, then turned back to Adam. "I'm looking for the captain of *The Rosslea*."

"And what do you want from him?" a man sitting at one of the back tables asked.

"That's between him and me," Evans said, "so unless you're him, I suggest you stay quiet."

"That would be me," a man said from the same table. He slurred his words.

"We can do this one of two ways: the fast way or the slow way," Evans said as he moved closer to the back table.

"What are you talking about? I have no quarrel with you."

"I beg to differ. Did you not say you was going to show my wife a thing or two?"

"I don't know your wife. Besides, I only have it in for one woman, and I assure you she would be no wife."

"That woman is my wife," Evans said as he finally reached the table.

"It's Captain Evans and *The Nitingale* crew!" one man shouted as he went to run for the door.

Pike stopped him with the butt of his gun. The rest of Evans's men pulled out their pistols and held the men still with them.

"Who are you?" the drunk captain asked.

"I'm Captain Evans, and I am here to kill you tonight."

"Wait just a minute," the man said. He tried to get up, but Evans pushed him back down. "Like I said to you, I don't know what it is you think I did to your wife. The woman I'm after is married to a man with a lot of money. She had her servant girl with her."

"Who told you that? Or was you there watching it all?"

"My man told me," he said. "Once he saw what happened, he ran to get me. That's when I spread the word that she is mine."

"Wrong," Evans said. "She's *mine*. The man who told you this—where is he?"

"That would be me," the man who Pike had hit with his pistol said. "I didn't know it was you, I swear I didn't."

The captain of *The Rosslea* began to laugh. "You mean to tell me that the woman who killed my brother was your wife? Well, that would make more sense anyway. I guess we have some unfinished business to attend to."

"I guess you're right. Let's get to it," Evans said with a smile on his face. "So tell me, do you want it easy or hard?"

"The hard way is best in my books, because by the time I get done with you, you'll be begging for me to kill you," the man said.

"I doubt that," he said as he pulled out his pistol. He shot the man before anything else could be said.

The crew of *The Rosslea* went into action.

Zack yelled out, "This is for Bre and her honor!"

Pike stabbed the man lying at his feet as he moved across the room to Zack's side.

Cliff was holding two men up against the wall. They felt helpless as their feet dangled above the ground and they struggled to get loose.

Donnie was in a punching match with a man, taking turns as if they were in a real boxing match for money.

Dean had a path of men lying on the floor, while Glover was at Evans's back, fighting.

While the rest of the men were locked into battle, Brandon was at the door taking out those men who tried to make a run for it.

Just then, the magistrate and his men came in, Richard following behind them. The magistrate fired his pistol to get everyone's attention.

The men came to a halt. Evans just smiled at Richard, who said, "I want to know what's going on here."

Spires told them that the crew of *The Rosslea* had started it all—that Captain Evans and his men were minding their own business, drinking and resting.

"Who is the captain of *The Rosslea*?" Richard asked.

"He's dead. This man killed him," a *The Rosslea* crew member said as he pointed at Evans.

"Then who's the second in command?" he asked, getting anger.

"That's me. How can I help you?" he asked before spitting out a mouthful of blood.

"What happened here? Why did your men attack?"

"We didn't, they did! We were getting ready to leave when they came in and started going on about his wife."

Kinkaid spoke up. "Are you really going to believe the word of a pirate over all these men you know?"

"A pirate? Everyone knows the penalty for being a pirate is," Richard said to the magistrate.

"Wait a minute. We're no more pirates than this ratty crew standing here with us. They're the most feared of the sea. So if you're going to hang us, they go as well!"

Evans and his crew busted out in laughter. They knew that if anything, they would spend the night in jail, and they could finish the job in there.

"Think about this: Do you really want them locked up with you?" Richard asked the man.

He turned around, then looked back up at him. "No, but if we hang, so do they."

"Look, I know these men who you're accusing. I can personally tell you that they are not pirates. Hell, they own this town, this tavern, this island. So let's go."

"What are you going to do with us?" the man asked the magistrate.

"Watch you all hang, and I guess you could say that your ship now belongs to the navy." He turned to Evans and his crew. "Men, I'm sorry that your night was disturbed. Please go back to drinking and carrying on. I'll get these men out of your way."

Richard walked over to Evans. "Nice pistols. I see that you done took them from your wife."

"No chance of that. They'll have to be back by the morning," Evans said with a smile.

Richard just laughed as he turned to leave.

After everyone cleared out, Glover walked over to Evans. "That was close. I can't tell you how bad I wanted to shoot him for running his mouth. Guess it's a good thing we're on the up-and-up."

"No, it's because he owns the island," Cliff said. "You never want to piss off the man who controls you."

"Boys," Evans called out. He looked at them; they were once again covered in blood. "It's time to sit and relax before we go home. Get you a bottle of rum and drink hearty."

"No, Bre will kill us," Zack said, Pike nodding his head in agreement.

"Hell, she's going to kill us all anyway once she finds out what happened here, so enjoy life while you got it," Brandon said before heading to the bar for a bottle of rum.

Just then Darrell walked in, looking around at the place and stopping at his son. "I see you did what you came for."

"Yes," Evans said, "and I'm sorry for the mess."

"Don't worry about that," he said. "Because you have until sunup to get this place cleaned up. If I was you, I'd get started." He turned and walked back out.

"So much for relaxing with a bottle of rum," Glover said.

"Aye, and they say I'm a hard man," Evans said with a laugh.

They turned around when they heard Cliff raising hell, then busted into laughter when they realized he was fussing over the billiards table being messed up.

By the time the sun came up, all the men were tired and in need of some rum. They'd rather fight all night and all day than have to clean up the tavern.

# Chapter 13

B re woke up the next morning and immediately noticed that Evans hadn't come home the previous night. She figured he was in the cave or on *The Nitingale*, sleeping off the rum, so she got dressed and went downstairs. As she walked into the kitchen, she saw that it was empty except for their new cook, who was fussing to herself about no one showing up for breakfast.

"What's wrong?" Bre asked her.

"Them chowhounds of yours didn't even show up this morning, and I fixed their favorites. See if I do that again."

Bre looked at her and then went out the door, leaving the cook to fuss. She went to the forge to ask Glover where everyone was. When she got there, she noticed that the walls were stripped and her new guns were gone.

The next step was clear: She needed to see where *The Nitingale* was. Once she got to the docks, she saw that the ship was gone. She knew something was going on, but she didn't know what. She stood there for a minute, then realized that if anyone knew where the men had gone, it would be Wendy. So she headed for her friend's rum shack.

Sure enough, Wendy was there, adding ingredients to the batch of rum she was making. "Good morning," Wendy said without looking up.

"Where are they?" Bre asked.

"Who?"

"Don't play with me. I know something's up, and you know what it is."

"They went to the big island to get supplies," Wendy said, moving to her work table.

"The ship was already stocked, so try again," Bre said as she moved closer to her friend.

"Bre, honey, calm down; it's nothing. All I know is that they went to the big island; they probably had some business to deal with, or they just decided to go into town and be men. That's what scares you, isn't it? Remember, they're used to hanging out at tavern's and drinking until the sun comes up. It's just one of those things we don't understand."

"Something isn't right, and I know it. So do you, but you're afraid to tell me, so it has to be bad—very bad."

"Stop overreacting. I'm sure they'll be back soon."

"Did you know they took all the weapons from the forge?" Bre asked as she sat down.

"Fine, you win," she said with a sigh. "They went into town to fight for you. Are you happy now?"

"What?"

"That man you killed, well, his brother put a price on your head. So our men went to take care of it."

Just then Cliff walked in and saw them talking. "Damn it, woman, can't you keep quiet for a day?" he asked Wendy.

"Not when she knew that you took all the weapons! How could I explain that?" Wendy asked him.

"Where's Evans?" Bre asked as she got up.

"Home," he answered.

"Thank you," she said, then left to go home and give them all hell.

Bre walked into the house carrying a bottle of rum. She found her family sitting at the table. The boys were eating and Evans was drinking out of his own bottle of rum. He looked up at her and said, "Thank you, I needed a good bottle of rum."

"Not this one. This one's mine," she said, getting a glass from the cupboard. She poured some rum into the glass as Evans got up to take it from her. Before he could reach for the glass, Bre just gave him a look that should the anger in her eyes.

"Princess," he said to her in a loving tone.

"We need to talk," she said as she looked at them, all covered in blood.

"Can I at least have the rum?" Evans asked.

Zack spoke up first. "We was just defending your honor, Sis. It wasn't that bad."

Pike looked at her with a grin. "It's your fault, you raised us this way."

Bre stared at them for a moment, then said softly, "Thank you, but I can take care of myself."

"Just be happy that we love you enough to kill for you," Brandon said.

This comment sent Bre over the edge into rage. She slammed her glass down, and went to pour her another glass.

"Nice going on that one," Pike said to his brother. "Look, what he meant was that we love you and we'd do anything to protect you, even kill for you."

Evans sat back and drank his rum, enjoying the fact that he wasn't getting yelled at.

And then Bre turned to him. "And you—where are my guns?"

"Right here, princess. They shot good; they don't need nothing done to them," he said with a smile.

Brandon looked at her. "You know, Sis, if you hadn't started any of this, we wouldn't have had to go and clean up after you."

As she started cussing at Brandon, she noticed that Evan, Pike, and, Zack were attempting to make a mad dash when they were stopped by their father.

"Breanna, that's enough. They did the only right thing to do, so stop this. If none of us loved you, we wouldn't care if some man wanted to see you dead. Just be thankful that they wouldn't let your old man go with them, or you might be getting us all out of jail."

She stopped and glared at them all before storming out of the kitchen. She went to the cave, where she knew she could calm down in peace.

Bob turned to his boys and Evans. "Brandon, next time, don't invoke her like that. You could've put it any other way."

"But it wouldn't be no different than how she would've told me."

"Maybe so, but remember, she's a lady, and she's always right, no matter how wrong she really is."

"Amen!" Evans said as he handed his father-in-law a glass of rum.

"Boys, you all did well. I couldn't be no prouder of you than I am right now. You've shown me that I made the right decision in letting you stay. Besides, Evans will need all the help with your sister he can get."

The boys looked at each other, speechless. This was the first time they'd been told that they could stay. They were thrilled that they wouldn't have to pull some kind of stunt to stay.

Evans disappeared to find Bre. He knew that she'd probably gone to the cave, so that was where he headed first. Sure enough, she was sitting in the sand at the opening, watching the waves come in.

"Are you still mad?" he asked as he sat down beside her.

"No, just hurt that you didn't tell me," Bre said as she put her head on his shoulder.

"I had my reasons."

"I know—you was afraid I'd go," she said with a faint laugh.

"No, I *knew* that you would," he said. "So am I forgiven?"

"Yes," she said, kissing him. "I could never stay to mad at you for long, but Brandon, on the other hand . . ."

"Let it go, princess. He loves you, and that's all that matters."

"Fine," she said, "only because he loves me, and I love him."

"Where's the baby?" Evans asked.

"Kandi has him. Why?" Bre asked with a questioning look.

"I thought I'd go to *The Nitingale* for some rest. Dad had us cleaning all night. We had to repair everything that got broken, and then I had to listen to Glover fuss about having to repair the weapons again. And Cliff was complaining all night because the billiard table was messed up."

Bre couldn't say anything, as she was too busy laughing. She laughed so hard that Evans was afraid she'd stop breathing.

"Come on, princess," he said once she'd calmed down. "I thought maybe you'd like to join me."

"Not until you take a swim," she said. "I'm not going anywhere until you wash all that blood off of you."

He looked down, seeming to realize for the first time that he was still covered in it. "Not a problem," he said. He jumped to his feet and picked her up. As she struggled and fussed, he jumped in.

"Why'd you do that?" she asked as she smiling at him.

"I might need help washing myself off," he said, smiling.

The next few days went by faster than she had wished. The men were getting ready to leave, as were her parents. She would soon be by herself until the beginning of storm season. She didn't like it much, but she knew it was safer here for her baby, than out there on the unpredictable sea.

Evans had encouraged the boys to pick a trade. Pike chose to learn blacksmithing, so he teamed up with Dean. Zack chose black-smithing as well, so Evans assigned him to Glover. Poor Brandon chose to learn to be a carpenter, and got stuck with Cliff, who had worked the boy's tail off getting things ready for their departure.

Evans also told them they needed to learn a special fighting skill. It worked out well for Pike and Zack because their trade teacher was also their skill teacher. Brandon, however, had to find time between Cliff and Donnie, who would teach him what he needed to know about fighting with cannons.

Bre went into town with Evans and the boys. Her parents were leaving, along with Kandi and her new beau, Shawn.

"Love you, Sis. Sorry I can't stay, but Dad needs me at home," Bobby told her. "Take care of our brothers and yourself. I can't wait to see my nephew." Then he got onto the ship.

Kandi came up with Shawn at her heels. "I hope you can make it to my wedding, whenever that might be. I might have to pull one of your stunts to get it to go faster," she whispered in Bre's ear. "I love you, and I'll miss you."

Then her parents came up. "We love you. Please try to keep them out of trouble," her mom said as she hugged her goodbye.

Her father said, "Remember what I told you, and everything will be fine." He hugged his daughter and joined the rest of his family on the ship.

"I wish they would've let me take them," Evans said.

"I think that one trip fixed them up for good," Bre said with a smile.

Later that night, once they were back home, the boys began pack-ing for the trip. While Evans got his stuff together and played with their son, he watched Bre, who was writing something.

He got up and walked over to her, then simply leaned over and took the sheet of paper from her.

"You can't read it until you're out to sea," she said, reaching out a hand to retrieve the letter.

"Have it your way. I wrote you one too, but I want you to read it now," he said, pulling a folded piece of paper from his pocket.

She took the note and looked at him, curious. Once she read the letter, she busted out in laughter. "Is this an order, Captain?"

"Yes."

"You really want me and the baby to go with you?"

"Well, I thought about it, and where I go, you go. Besides, you was the one who said the safest place was at my side."

"You're only doing this because you're afraid I'll get into trouble while you're gone."

"A little," he said, then changed the subject. "Do you want to take Olivia to help you with the baby, or someone else?"

"I'll ask her," Bre said. "I love you." She stood to leave, then stopped. "We can't do that; we don't have anywhere to put her."

"Well, that was a surprise for you. I had Cliff do some remodeling on *The Nitingale*. We cut our room a little to make another room for the baby and a nanny. I knew that when this day came, we would need it. Because I wasn't leaving you."

"Then I guess that works out good." Bre smiled at him.

"What do you mean?" Evans looked at her.

"I knew you'd do this, so I already had my bags packed," she said with a small smile. "Besides, after the last time you went without me, you said, 'Never again.'"

"I love you," he said, moving in to kiss her.

"And I love you, Captain."

The rest of the season was uneventful. They had no trouble to deal with. Before they were to head home, they stopped in Oracoke for some supplies. When they pulled up, they noticed that Hoss was there as well.

Evans watched as the men were tying the sails down, then walked over to Bre. "I'm proud of our boys," he said to her.

She smiled. "I am too."

Hoss was sitting in the tavern at a back table, trying to enjoy his rum while listening to his crew tell stories about *The Nitingale* and how special she was.

"This is bullshit. A man can't even come in here and enjoy a good bottle of rum or two without listening to stories about Evans and his almighty ship. What makes her so special anyway? She's just a wooden ship like mine," Hoss said to Ronnie.

But it was Evans who answered him. "Well, it's because she's mine." He smacked his brother on the back. "Stop being so hateful; you're part of their conversation."

"Aye, I know," he said. "So what brings you here?"

"We needed some supplies, and then we're heading home for the season. What about you?"

"The same. Those are some nice pistols in your belt. Where'd you steal them from?"

"I got these from Richard, but if you think these are nice, you need to see Bre's. Her set's the best."

Just then they heard the barkeep talking to some men. "No, I heard she's made from sixty acres of haunted forest, and that her men are immortal. That's why they can't be killed."

"That's all right; I heard she came straight from hell, and that her crew works for the devil himself," Mike added.

"No, it's that she's impossible to sink and that her crew works for Calypso. That way, when they don't fall for her game, she sends them out," some man in the back said.

"Think about it like this," Hoss said to the crowd. "If she's all that, then why are men talking about it? If she was all that, she wouldn't leave survivors; no one would be here talking about her. If that was my ship, I know I wouldn't leave survivors."

Suddenly a man ran into the place. "It's not safe here. She's in the docks; we need to get to safety!"

The men busted out in laughter and returned to drinking and talking about *The Nitingale* and her almighty crew.

Hoss just looked at Evans. "You are loving all of this. What makes her so special?"

"Love, my friend, it's all love. We love her, take care of her, and baby her. In return, she takes care of all of us."

"Can't argue with that one. So when are you leaving?"

"Just as soon as I get back on the ship," Evans answered. "When are you?"

"As soon as I finish this bottle," Hoss said with a smile. "Got to get home. Austin's driving me mad, and I miss Roe."

"Well, drink up," Evans said, laughing.

Once the men pulled up to the island, they both simultaneously fired their cannons to let the island know they were home.

Suddenly, another shot came from behind them—it was Steven.

"Perfect timing," Evans said to Bre. "We're all home. Means for a good party." Once they pulled in, they saw that Jerry, Jim, and Ray were already there. "All my family is home, safe and sound."

The next day, as the men were all catching up, Bre and the women prepared for the end-of-year party. She was happy to be home, but she missed the rocking of the ship. Her baby was walking and talking.

She knew it wouldn't be long before he be growing up too fast for her liking, but she would handle that when it came.

Later that night, while everyone was gathering together, Bre looked over to her husband. "I love you, my love. Thank you for everything."

"No, thank you, my love. Without you, I would be lost forever." He pulled a folded-up piece of paper from his pocket. "You know, I never read your note." He unfolded it and studied it for a moment.

*My Darling Captain,*

*The sea is a part of you, as you are a part of it. The mighty* Nitingale *will take care of you once again, so take good care of her. I will keep my eyes on the horizon, waiting for you. I will pray every night for your return, with whispers of love sent to you over the sea. For I know, no matter where you are, I am with you. Where you go, I go, forever and always.*

"You knew you was going with me. So why'd you write this?"

"Well, it's like this: I knew I was going one way or another. Either by you taking me, or me sneaking onto the ship," she said with a smile.

"What am I going to do with you?" he asked as his father walked up.

"Thanks to you two, I had to suffer through a huge investigation to show that we wasn't pirates. They hanged them men last week, so they won't give us any more problems."

"What do you mean, investigation?" Hoss asked as he and his crew approached the group.

"They wouldn't keep quiet. They kept telling everyone, including the judge, that we were pirates. So they had to investigate CP and Trading."

"What's this about? What men?" Steven asked as he and his crew joined in.

"Well, boys," Evans said to them, "Bre got into trouble in town."

"I did not. I got into a fight in town, and won. Thank you," she added.

"Anyway, the man she killed—his brother sent word that he was going to kill her. So we took care of it."

"After we was accused of being pirates," Glover said. "Can you believe that? Us, pirates?"

All the men busted out laughing.

"To make a long story short, they fought for my honor and got caught by the magistrate, who arrested the other men, while they were crying and carrying on about us being pirates. Then Darrell came and made them clean up the tavern," she said to them.

"So you went off and had more fun without us," Steven said. "Since when do you get to have all the fun?"

"Shut up," Hoss said. "How bad was Bre hurt?"

"I wasn't," she said. "All I got was a black eye."

"And a busted pistol," Glover added.

Jerry, Ray, and Jim all just laughed. "Yep, I told you I need a woman like that." Jerry said as he was laughing.

"A woman like that just about made us all hang. If it wasn't for the fact that I keep two sets of books, we would've been had," Darrell told them.

"You can't blame me," Bre said. "If Evans had stayed home and left things alone, none of this would've happened."

Brandon spoke up. "No, if that damn magistrate would've stayed home, then we would've killed them all, and that would've been it."

Austin looked at Pike and Zack. "Just how many men have you killed?"

"Well, we haven't kept count, but I'd say a good dozen or so apiece," Zack answered.

"The important thing is that we're still here to tell about it," Pike added.

Austin looked at his dad. "See, if you would've left me with Evans, I could be as good as them."

"Hell, no," Hoss said. "Now get out of here; these two are like a damn magnet for trouble." He pointed to Bre and Evans.

"Yes, I'm definitely going to have to find me a woman like her to kidnap," Jerry said again as he walked off with some of the others.

"Don't worry about that," Evans said to Hoss. "The boys are going with you next season. I'm done, and they need to learn."

Steven spoke up. "Why him?"

"Because we know he won't kill them," Bre said before walking away.

"That's not fair," Steven said with a laugh. "Everyone gets to have all the fun, and I'm stuck getting the blame for it."

"We love you too, Steven," Bre said as she disappeared out the door.

"Great," Hoss said as he turned to Evans, "so I get to have the young cutthroats while Steven gets off scot-free. That doesn't seem right to me."

"Better you than me," Steven said. "This way you can have the headache. Plus, they'd tell Evans and Bre everything I did wrong."

Hoss just stared at him and then turned back to Evans. "What about your crew, are they splitting up?"

"Not a chance," Glover said. "We're staying at his side. That way, if something happens, we're here for him.

Evans went into the great hall and held up his glass. "I would like to make a toast."

Everyone became quiet and turned to him. Bre walked in from outside, looking up at him.

"This is to all my men. Without you, this would not be possible. I just hope that we have more fun and adventure yet to come. Here's to another great season. And knowing my wife and my crew, we'll need all the luck we can get for the next season."

"Hear, hear," everyone called out before returning to dancing and talking.

Bre walked over to her husband. "I'm not that bad."

"No, but you are that mean."

She just smiled and said, "You win this time, but I'm telling you, one day I will."

"I love you, princess." He kissed her softly.

"And I love you, Captain Evans."

"I need a word with the both of you," Darrell interrupted, then took them to the office.

A little boy about three years old. He had beautiful curly blonde hair, and the biggest set of bright blue eyes, stood inside. Bre looked at him, then back at Darrell and Evans. "Who's this?"

"This little boy is my grandson," Darrell said.

Evans saw the fire in Bre's eyes, then watched it pass when she turned back to the boy. She went over to him and picked him up. "Well, let's go and introduce you to your brother." She turned to her husband. "We'll talk about this later." Then she asked Darrell, "What's his name?"

"His name is Scott, and he's almost five."

Bre smiled at him, then walked over to her husband. "This, Scott, is your father."

"Bre——" Evans began, but she stopped him.

"This is our family. It doesn't matter what happened before me, my love."

"I love you," he said, gazing at her.

"Let's introduce him to the boy's." She smiled as she went toward the door.

Jim watched them as they walked off. "Well I lost that bet," he said to Darrell.

"Me too," he replied. "Look at that family. My son is one lucky man."

"Aye, he is," Jim said as he watched with a smile.

# About the Author

LeeAnna Neece was raised in central Florida and now lives in northeastern Tennessee with her husband, who also happens to be her best friend. A mother of four as well as a grandmother, Neece loves animals, traveling, and history. She spends her free time playing billiards, out and about with her husband on his Harley, or spending quality time with friends and family. *Isle of Innocence* is her second book and is a sequel to her first, *A Captive Heart*.